From the Mystical Beyond

From the Mystical Beyond

Cave of Shiva

Kalki and the First Awakening

Partho

ink | kãli

ISBN: 978-93-6547-521-0

Cover design by Geetanjali

First published in India 2025
This edition published 2025

BluOne Ink Pvt. Ltd
A-76, 2nd Floor, Sector 136, Noida
Uttar Pradesh 201301
www.bluone.ink
publisher@bluone.ink

Printed and bound in India by Thomson Press (India) Ltd

Kali and Occam are imprints of BluOne Ink

'In my view, a man's value does not depend on what he learns, or his position or fame, or what he does, but on what he is and inwardly becomes.'

—Sri Aurobindo

Contents

II Kalki and the First Awakening

A Brief Note on the Cover Image

The image depicts Kalki, the feminine avatar of the new age, arising out of the blue waters of creation (or manifestation), wearing a crown of golden fire, ascending upward towards the highest heavens, symbolizing the evolutionary ascent of human consciousness into the Divine. Behind Kalki is the Shivalinga—the mystic portal to Shiva's secret Cave, the hriday guhayam of the Upanishads.

Adi

How do you introduce a book that tells you to abandon everything you know? A book that, if followed closely, leaves you wordless, speechless, thoughtless.

This is often what happens to me after a conversation with Partho. The mind gives up its adherence to the 'known'. And something unknown begins to happen. What is this unknown? It would not be 'unknown' if I were to attempt a description of it. You will have to explore it for yourself.

And who is Partho? I know that he is my friend—*and I cannot say, how long, for that is to place it in time*—but he needs no introduction, because he has none. There was a time when I used to call him the finest teacher of Vedanta of our times. Then I began calling him one of the greatest minds of the last century. But if you read him, you will see that he defies all labels.

In a play I once wrote about him, I suggested that he was Partho-everything. Then I realized he was Partho-nothing. Eventually, I settled on the notion that he might be Wholo-nothing. But then, even that would be missing the truth.

Let us talk about the book, then, since we clearly have not understood anything about the author with all my Vedantic deconstructions. We can say a few things about the book, though even those may be arguable.

The first part, 'Cave of Shiva', seems to be a story. But is it really a story? It seems more like a journey. But whose journey? The author's or someone else's? Is it a true story? Or fiction? Or both? I do not know. Is it magical realism? Is it fantasy? A spiritual narrative? It seems to be a story about nothing, and everything. An Upanishadic dialogue that collapses the foundations we build in life to find stability, and questions our reliance on arbitrary concepts, words and meanings, superficial phrases, until we realize that we have been living an illusion, surrounded by a deep fear—a fear of letting falsehood go, and clinging to rays of light that pass through our fingers. It is the fear of truth.

This is why the book is so precious to me. Not because it offers answers, but because it resolves questions that have no meaning. But I do not wish to break your suspense and reveal everything I do not know about the book. I invite you to find out for yourself. Perhaps then you will realize the fundamental difficulty I described in my opening line: How do you describe that which takes you beyond words?

The second part, 'Kalki and the First Awakening', is even more enigmatic.

Who is this Kalki, creating herself and giving birth so that she can transform life at its roots? We do not know, though the author gives us a few clues about who this might be.

Perhaps the Mother of Pondicherry Ashram, who attempted a radical—and arguably the most far-reaching—experiment on earth, an experiment still unravelling, not yet complete. And, maybe, you and I are meant to complete it by creating ourselves in a new light and vision, by bringing self-transformation to a point where it becomes a tipping point for evolution on earth.

Is that even possible? Or just a fantasy? But then again, whatever we believe it to be, that it becomes. If we believe it is inevitable, it is. If we call it magical realism, that too. And why not? If evolution is to be creative, then each of us must have the freedom and the responsibility to design it as we will.

Pariksith Singh, MD

A student and exponent of Hindu Dharma, and one who has been deeply engaged spiritually and intellectually with Sri Aurobindo and his Yoga for almost all his adult life, Dr Singh is the author of *Sri Aurobindo and the Literary Renaissance of India* (2021), *Sri Aurobindo and Philosophy* (2022) and *The Veda Made Simple* (2023).

I

Cave of Shiva

About the Story

'Cave of Shiva' is not a work of yogic or Vedantic philosophy but a story about a great sage who lived all his life in Shiva's consciousness, in the purest inner silence, and in complete anonymity. He came from his native state of Bengal to the Himalayas when he was in his early twenties, and then stayed on in the Himalayas, in a house near an ancient Shiva temple, for more than forty years, absorbed in his all-consuming quest for the Divine. No one knew his name nor his origins beyond the fact that he was from Bengal. He hardly met people and spoke to no one. Most of the villagers who would come to the temple would only see glimpses of him, and only a rare few, enormously privileged, would receive his direct blessings. Everyone referred to him as Mauni Baba. *Mauni* means one who is silent, and *Baba* is a term of respect used for ascetics, or elderly men. In later years, he came to be called simply *Babaji*.

With the passing years, Babaji became more and more of a recluse, and the few visits he would make to the temple also ceased. Then, eventually, Babaji disappeared from human sight. No one knew where he had gone, but he had gone. His little room adjoining the temple was found abandoned. The villagers discovered a single wooden cot, a table and a chair, and some books on a shelf. There was only one framed picture of Sri Aurobindo hanging on the wall above the shelf. In one corner of the room, there was a small stove, a couple of plates, a jug, a couple of glasses and spoons, and an earthen water pot on a wooden stand. This was the barest of bare rooms.

For many years, the villagers, and especially those who were touched and blessed by him over the years, kept looking for him wherever they went. But no one found him, or any traces of him. Gradually, everyone forgot about the Mauni Baba.

And then, many years later, a young man from the city of Delhi, came up to the abandoned temple, curious to learn about this mysterious Babaji. He found Babaji's old, abandoned room and the ruins of the temple. He went into the room and looked for some sign of Babaji. No one knows what or who he found. Perhaps, no one will ever know. But when this young man came back, he believed that he had met Babaji and had spent a whole night and day with him. He confided this rather mysterious bit of information only to his companion. His companion, in turn, did not share this with anyone. She continued to live with this young man for many years.

Only in her advanced years, she shared her story with another living person, a young disciple of hers, on the understanding that he would not make this public for as long as she was in her body. He kept that understanding.

This is Babaji's story. But much more than that, this is the story of a young man who was directly given the touch of Shiva through the mysterious Babaji. This is also, at another level, the story of a young woman who got the touch of Shiva from the man she loved and adored as her soulmate, her sahadharmi. But finally, this is our story—the story of each one of us who seeks in the depths of our minds and hearts the touch of Shiva.

The Dream and the Trek

There is an ancient, dilapidated Shiva temple somewhere beyond Almora in the Kumaon range of the upper Himalayas. To reach the temple, you have to climb about 10,000 feet to a remote village, and then take a narrow hilly detour, used many years ago by only the local village people, towards the temple. Not too many city people know of this temple. It is neither a tourist attraction nor a pilgrimage. For that matter, not even the local villagers visit that temple anymore. No one would want to climb a thousand odd feet to visit a ruin.

Our story is about this temple, and about a young man who saw this temple in a dream. His name was Adi. *Adi* means the first, the original. Adi was the only son of a wealthy *zamindar*, or landowner, who had once, while still a teenager, wanted to become a *sadhu*, a wandering monk. Fortunately, for everyone involved, he met a very pragmatic guru, who owned an ashram by the Ganga near Rishikesh, who advised him to exhaust his worldly *samskaras* before embracing the life of a renunciant. No one knows for sure what the guru had seen in Adi's father or why he had advised him to postpone monkhood. Adi's father, however, being a rather simple-minded person, had no such questions, and obeyed his guru immediately. He went back to the worldly life, found himself a woman worthy of his love and adoration, and went on to double his ancestral wealth. But, despite all the worldly life and its attractions, he could never fully exhaust his sadhu-samskaras, and somewhere deep in his soul, the desire to become a sadhu remained dormant.

There is a belief amongst Hindus that whatever desire you hold long enough in your heart comes true, in this or some other lifetime. But occasionally, the desire gets driven down into your DNA and then assumes the living form of your offspring. Strange are the ways of karma.

Adi was born at six in the morning of Mahashivratri, the day Hindus dedicate to Shiva, a day of fasting, praying and meditation. And, even as Adi's mother lay in bed anticipating the birth of her child in the next few hours, Adi's father dreamed of Shiva. As he woke up, with the dream still fresh in his mind, he was told that his wife had given birth to a boy. Everyone in the family celebrated—this was doubly auspicious: the birth of a child at six on the morning of Mahashivratri, and the fact that the father had dreamt of Shiva in the hours preceding the birth.

≈

Adi was twenty-four when he had his first dream of the temple.

He was climbing a narrow grassy path through a thickly forested hill when he glimpsed the temple looming a few hundred feet above him. It was built out of solid rock, with a very low and small wooden door leading into it. For just a second, he saw a tall human figure inside the temple, bathed in a deep red glow. And then it all disappeared.

Adi woke up with a start, almost expecting to find himself climbing that forested hill. But obviously, there was no hill, no forest, no temple. Adi was sitting on his bed, staring at the walls of his room, his heart still pounding away. He looked at the watch on his bedside table. It showed 3 am.

≈

Adi wasn't particularly interested in temples, or religion—he was a student of literature and philosophy, and a cultivated skeptic. There was no outer reason for him to dream of the temple. But the dream was so vivid that he was compelled to take it more seriously than he would take any other dream. That evening, when he met with Ira, his childhood friend and companion, he shared the dream with her. She was a writer and freelance editor, with an abiding passion for mythology. The temple, as Adi described to her, immediately caught her interest.

'Maybe this temple actually exists somewhere,' she said wistfully.

'Maybe,' Adi agreed.

But then, they forgot about the dream. And the days went by.

≈

A year later, Adi dreamed again of the temple.

This time, he was much closer to the temple. He was standing under a huge tree, on a stony platform, looking at the ancient rock-hewn temple. A small and narrow door led into it. There was a deep red glow inside the temple. He felt irresistibly drawn towards it. As he started walking up the stony steps leading to the temple, he glimpsed—just for the briefest moment—the human figure again, looming next to the temple entrance. And then, once again, everything disappeared.

≈

When he shared his second dream with Ira, she was far more intrigued. 'Why would you dream of this temple a second time unless there is some occult significance?' She asked Adi.

Adi, aware of her keen interest in occultism and mythology, nodded. Not that he entirely accepted her reasoning. 'The first time around, I didn't pay so much attention, though the dream, in its vividness, was unlike any other I've had. But a second time?'

'And it was vivid this time too…' Ira added.

'Almost as if I was actually there!' Adi said emphatically.

'You know I'm very good at sketching, don't you?' She asked, struck by inspiration.

Adi nodded.

'So, why don't you describe the temple to me, exactly as it came to you, and I will try sketch it.'

That was the beginning of the odyssey.

The sketch that Ira drew was a remarkably faithful rendering of the image of the temple in Adi's dreams. When Adi saw her work, he couldn't help gasping in astonishment. 'Exactly as I saw it in my dreams!' he exclaimed.

'So now let's get down to some digging. Let me see if something like this actually exists somewhere!'

It took them four months of research to locate the temple in the real world. They found it in the interior of the Himalayas, deep in a mountain forest, along a long forgotten, abandoned trek to a glacier. Once they had identified the temple—supposedly a thousand years old—it took them just a couple of weeks to find a group of trekkers interested in a trek to the glacier. Ira's friend Deva, an avid trekker, offered to take care of organizing the details of the trek. Two of Ira's close friends, John Shotton, an English teacher, and Monica, a journalist, joined them for the trek. Adi and Ira did not reveal the real purpose of the trek to anyone. They themselves were not too sure of where the trek would lead.

Their destination was Pindari Glacier, at a height of 11,800 feet, in the upper reaches of the Kumaon Himalayas. They had taken the local bus from Almora, a bustling mountain town, to a small village called Saung, the last motorable point for the trek. It was late evening by the time they got to Saung, both tired and excited. They had pre-booked all the guest houses along the way and their first overnight stop was at the small government rest house, a rather dilapidated structure that didn't look too welcoming. But none of them cared much; they were too focused on the trek the next morning.

There were two caretakers and a dog. The dog was friendly and noisy. The caretakers were quiet and sullen. They only brightened up a bit when they were offered a drink of the local rum. The caretakers lit a campfire and went off to cook a meal. The four of them sat around the fire and sipped their drinks, quiet, as if conserving their energies for the eight-day trek ahead. They also knew that there would be very few rest houses or villages along the way.

The night was restful, though cold, and the rooms, to their pleasant surprise, were cozy and comfortable. They fell asleep quickly and woke up early, enjoyed the luxury of a bath, quite aware that there would be no baths for the next ten days, and dressed for the trek. Each of them was carrying a backpack and a walking stick—the backpacks as light as they could make it, and the sticks indispensable on a trek. They had a simple local breakfast, paid the caretakers, and left the rest house just as it was getting a bit warm and sunny. The dog followed them for a good kilometer or two and then turned back, obviously quite used to escorting trekkers back and forth.

They started the climb at exactly half past eight, looking forward to an exciting high-altitude trek.

≈

They were four days into the trek, and had climbed to nearly 10,500 feet, when they reached base camp, a very small village called Phurkia—really a cluster of a few huts, the last break before climbing the final thousand feet to the glacier. There was a small government rest house just outside the village which they had booked for two days. This was the last village and the last rest house on the trek. Beyond this were the mountainous ranges of the higher Himalayas, snow covered all the year, freezing cold.

The caretaker of the rest house was himself an expert trekker and often used to take groups to the glacier. He was going to take this small group too to the glacier the next morning. He lit a campfire for them, and the friends sat around it, thankful for the warmth. As the sun went down, it suddenly became dark and cold. The starlit sky was breathtaking—and the stars all seemed within an arm's distance, as if you could just reach out and touch them.

'So, habitation finishes here?' Adi asked the caretaker as he warmed his palms over the fire.

'Yes Sir,' the caretaker replied. 'There's no habitation beyond this village, except for an old house, about an hour's climb from here. And an abandoned temple no one visits anymore.'

That was what Adi was waiting for. 'The thousand-year-old Shiva temple?'

'Maybe older than that, Sir,' the caretaker said. 'They say it has been there for more generations than anyone can recall. Older than the Jageshwar temples.'

'Oh,' Adi exclaimed, keenly interested. 'And the house? Does someone live there?'

'Yes Sir,' the caretaker said. 'Babaji. It's his ashram.'

'Who's Babaji?' Adi asked, further intrigued.

'An old yogi, Sir,' said the caretaker. 'He came here to the village many years ago. Most of the villagers don't remember when. The eldest of the village, who passed away last year, remembered that he was a kid of ten or so when Babaji arrived here in this village—a young man with flowing black hair.'

'How old was this "eldest" when he passed?' Adi asked.

The caretaker shrugged. 'Oh, we wouldn't know. Eighty, perhaps?'

Adi did a quick calculation. 'That would make Babaji very old indeed!'

'At least a hundred twenty, Sir!'

'Are you sure this is not some mountain legend?' Adi asked. 'Has anyone met Babaji of late?'

By now everyone else was tuned into the conversation as well, all of them intrigued too.

The caretaker thought for a moment and said, 'No, Sir, not that I know of.'

'So, how do we know that Babaji still lives in his ashram?'

'We don't, Sir!' said the caretaker.

'Then it may well be a legend?'

The caretaker kept quiet, a bit pensive. The fire crackled in the overwhelming quietude of the night. Nothing else stirred. Adi had not experienced such dense quietude before.

And then, suddenly, a thought seemed to float into Adi's consciousness—*Why not find out for yourself?* He felt a sudden shiver run up his spine.

He looked at the caretaker and said after a long pause—'Can I go there? Can you give me the directions?'

'Hey!' Monica looked quizzically at Adi. 'Seriously?'

Deva spoke up immediately. 'Adi, we have one single day to go to the glacier and come back. That itself will take us the whole day!'

Adi asked the caretaker—'Can I go and come back tomorrow itself? If I don't go to the glacier?'

'Don't go to the glacier—?' repeated Monica. 'We have come here for the glacier, Adi!'

'Hey guys,' Adi said, looking earnestly at the group. 'I came for the trek, and for some exploration. I have enjoyed the trek so far, and I will enjoy my exploration too. Can I go to the temple while you guys go up to the glacier?'

'Let him go,' Ira said quietly. 'He'll be back before us.'

'Yes, I'll be back long before you all.' Adi said confidently. 'I would rather visit the temple than the glacier. I mean,

I have seen glaciers. They all look and feel the same. This temple will be very different.'

While his companions looked uncertainly at one another, Adi turned to the caretaker. 'How far did you say it was?'

'Not too far, Sir,' the caretaker said. 'It's a straight trek up for about an hour at your speed. At my speed, perhaps forty or forty-five minutes.'

'In kilometers?' asked Adi.

'Oh, about six,' the caretaker said with a shrug.

'A steep climb?'

'For about half the way, and then it levels out more or less.'

'Can I go alone? No chance of getting lost on the way?'

'Sure, Sir,' the caretaker replied. 'No one can get lost. It's a straight climb. And you will see the ashram as soon as you take a couple of turns up the hill.'

'So, that's decided,' Adi declared with a flourish. 'I shall go and pay Babaji a visit. The rest of you can enjoy the glacier!'

≈

Adi went out alone after dinner to smoke a cigar. He found a big boulder right behind the rest house and climbed on to it. He sat on it and lit his cigar. He inhaled a few quick puffs. It was good! He closed his eyes, taking in the dense silence around him. Somewhere in the distance he could hear the soft murmurs of a river. As he took a long puff, he felt a slight movement beside him. He turned and saw Ira.

'Not disturbing, I hope?' she asked softly.

'Nope,' Adi said. 'Join me.' He moved aside and made place for her on the boulder. She climbed and sat down next to him, placing her gloved hand on his knee.

'Adi,' she said softly, 'are you sure you want to go alone? You know, we can extend our trip by a day, and we can all go and see this temple of yours together, maybe the day after?'

'Hey, no,' Adi said immediately. 'Firstly, that will be a logistical nightmare—we will have to change all our rest house bookings and that would mean someone going down all the way specially for this. And secondly, I don't want everyone with me when I go to the temple and probably meet this Babaji!'

'You'll be good on your own?' she asked.

'Yes, Ira,' Adi replied, taking her hand firmly in his. 'I need to do this, and on my own. You enjoy the glacier with your friends and bring me back some pictures. And I will probably bring back some pictures of the venerable Babaji and the temple!' Adi said, smiling.

'You think he's still there?' she asked.

Adi puffed at the cigar. 'I have no idea,' he said. 'These babas have all kinds of extraordinary powers. You never know.'

She smiled a bit ruefully. 'Will miss you on the trek!'

'Oh, just one day, my dear!' He smiled at her. 'We will enjoy our trek back together!'

'Well, goodnight, then. Love you!'

'Love you too! Sleep well!'

Adi closed his eyes again as Ira left.

Babaji and the Old House

Early morning, next day. It was bitterly cold, but there was crisp sunlight. The caretaker said it would be a pleasant day, not too cold, not too breezy. The climb should be comfortable.

Ira, Deva, Monica and John, along with the caretaker, left immediately for the final lap of the trek after breakfast so that they could return in good time. Adi left a bit later, taking the narrow mountain path towards the ashram and the temple. The climb was gentle at first and then got steeper. The higher he climbed, the more beautiful the view got. The breeze too grew stronger. Adi climbed uphill for about half an hour after which the ground levelled out. In about ten minutes, he could see a small house in the distance with some tall trees around it. It was exactly as the caretaker had described the ashram building. A narrow path climbed gently towards it. He was now enjoying the sunlight and the breeze.

It took him another quarter of an hour to reach the old house, Babaji's ashram. It was a small stone cottage with a few big boulders and tall trees around it. The cottage looked old but not dilapidated. He could see a few stone steps leading up to a large wooden door at the entrance of the house. He climbed the steps to the wooden door and knocked on it. The door opened inward with a slight creaking sound. It had obviously been left open. Adi stepped in gingerly, not too sure what to expect.

It was dimly lit, dry and cool inside. There was no one in sight. Adi could make out a source of light at the far end of the room. He walked towards it and came to a small door, again left ajar, which opened out to a patio. There was a wooden reclining chair and a small table beside it. Beyond the patio, he could see a mountain stream running below the house. Between the house and the stream was a large patch of vegetation.

There was no sign of anyone living there. It was quiet as a tomb. Adi turned around and walked back into the stone cottage. He could see no item of furniture, no book, no baggage. Nothing. He felt disappointed. This was an abandoned building, and there was no Babaji.

Adi went back to the patio and sat on the abandoned chair. He felt tired and decided to rest for a while before starting the trek back to the rest house. He reckoned that the walk back, which would be all downhill, wouldn't take more than forty minutes or so, and it was just 11 am by his watch. He closed his eyes, taking in the gentle and steady sound of the stream, and feeling the warmth of the sun on his face. Before he knew it, he was asleep.

≈

He could feel someone beside him. He wasn't too sure if he was still asleep or awake. With some effort of the will, he opened his eyes. The sun was about to set, and the breeze felt cold on his skin. The sound of the river seemed a bit louder. He sat up with a start. *Oh, God—how do I go back?*

And then Adi saw him right beside him, wearing a white dhoti and a shawl wrapped around his upper body. He was clean shaven with long, shoulder-length hair. He looked young and fresh, not a year older than forty. His eyes were like coals burning in the dark. Adi had never seen eyes that intense. The man seemed quite out of place there, in that abandoned house in the Himalayan wilderness. He would have fitted in comfortably in a city temple or even a university.

'Babaji?' Adi asked quietly.

'Yes,' the man replied in English. Adi was taken aback. This man—or Babaji?—looked superbly calm, completely at ease. He looked at Adi as if it was the most normal thing in the world to find a stranger sleeping in one's patio.

'I am sorry,' Adi spluttered, not knowing how to explain his presence in the house. 'I wanted to meet you, to find out if you were here at all.' He ended somewhat lamely.

He smiled, a very kind and infectious smile. 'I know,' he said softly, a bit effeminately perhaps. 'I was expecting you.'

Adi couldn't comprehend that. *How could he be expecting me?* But then, Babaji was supposed to be a yogi, and yogis are supposed to know things. Babaji kept looking at Adi, keen interest and compassion in his eyes.

Adi stood up, feeling no apprehension, no nervousness, very much at ease. Adi instinctively knew that it was something to do with Babaji's presence.

He bowed to Babaji. 'Pranam, Babaji!' He said respectfully.

Babaji placed his right hand on Adi's head and said, '*Ayushman bhava*. And you may call me Shiva. Babaji makes me feel ancient!'

'Shiva? Is that your name?' Adi asked.

'It's the name I gave myself,' Babaji said, 'when I realized my identity with him.'

'Realized your identity with Shiva?' Adi repeated, both awe and incredulity in his voice.

'Yes,' said Babaji matter-of-factly.

'Oh!' That was all Adi could say after that. *Realized his identity with Shiva*. Who on earth can say a thing like that? Either a madman, a megalomaniac, or...? Adi could not complete his thought—he suddenly remembered that he needed to get back to Phurkia before dark. 'I have some friends waiting for me at the rest house in Phurkia, Babaji...I mean, Shivaji... and it's already pretty late.'

Shivaji didn't sound quite right.

'Don't worry,' Babaji said, smiling. 'All that is already taken care of. Stay here for the night and you can go back tomorrow. Your friends will be waiting for you.' From Babaji's accent, Adi could easily make out that he was educated and cultured.

'Already taken care of?' Adi repeated slowly, not certain what that meant.

Babaji did not respond to that question. Instead, saying—'You must be hungry, let's eat something,' he walked back into the house. Adi followed, thankful for the invitation, though still very intrigued by it all.

'And yes, *Shivaji* didn't sound right,' he heard Babaji saying with a chuckle.

The room inside was now illumined by a lamp that sat on a table in the corner. The room looked and felt much larger now.

"Shiva" motioned Adi to sit on the floor. Adi quickly glanced down and saw two thick rugs on the floor.

'I'll be back,' Shiva said and went out again. He came back in a few minutes with a small bowl which he then placed in front of Adi. The bowl had red rice with nuts and fruits in it. It was a very small portion, but it was something at least, and Adi was ravenous. He looked up at Shiva—where was *his* food?

'I eat only once a day,' Shiva said, anticipating his question. 'So have your fill.'

Adi didn't mind that the portion was certainly not large enough for him to have 'his fill' but started eating, as if it were a feast. The portion of the red rice and fruits was over in no time, but it was delicious. *This is a bit of miracle,* Adi thought to himself—*how can he prepare something so damned delicious out of just rice and some nuts and fruits?* But there was a greater miracle happening that took a few more minutes to register. He did not want a repeat, he was full—he couldn't have eaten a single morsel more. Total satiation. *How the hell?*

Shiva chuckled, as if he could hear Adi thinking. 'Don't try to figure out things, Adi. I'm glad you enjoyed the food!'

Adi? How did he know my name, Adi thought. *I didn't tell him. He never asked. But what the heck—either I am still dreaming, sitting on that very comfortable chair and listening to the river, or I am in the presence of a yogi, and miracles are in order.*

'Want to go for a walk, Adi?' Shiva asked gently. 'Get some cold night air?'

'Of course, Sir,' Adi sounded eager. 'And we can talk, if you don't mind—I have so many questions!'

A Walk in the Starlight

It was cold, and the breeze had picked up considerably. The starlit sky was awesome. They could see the way before them perfectly in that bright starlight. The two of them walked ever so quietly, overwhelmed by the ethereal beauty of the night. Shiva's presence was comforting, solid, like the Himalayas. Everything seemed exactly the way it was meant to be, not a pebble out of place. The sound of the mountain stream in the background blended ever so perfectly with the silence of the mountain. The crunch of an occasional twig under their feet was the only sound that could dare break the awesome quietude.

'Shiva, do you live alone here?' Adi asked a bit cautiously, still a bit hesitant calling him by that name.

'Alone?' he shot back. 'But everyone is alone.'

Adi had never known a yogi before and had no idea how they lived, thought or spoke.

'May I ask a question, Sir?' Adi asked, wanting to make sure that Shiva wouldn't consider his curiosity a nuisance or an intrusion.

'By all means,' Shiva said amiably. 'We have the whole night.'

And indeed, it felt that they had the whole night. Adi did not feel the least bit tired but filled with eager curiosity, fully aware that he was in the presence of an extraordinary being.

'Babaji,' Adi began conversationally, and stopped. 'Sorry—I mean Shiva.'

Shiva smiled.

'They say you have been living here for many years,' Adi continued. 'No one seems to remember when you came.'

'Ah, yes,' said Shiva, 'that's because I don't meet anyone now. There was a time I used to go down to the villages every winter when it used to get very cold up here. And some villagers used to come up here to check out on me and bring me all kinds of stuff. Now, it's different. Perhaps they find it more difficult to come.'

'But I could come up here rather easily,' said Adi.

Shiva smiled. 'You came up because I put the thought into your head, Adi!'

'Oh,' said Adi, remembering the thought that had suddenly popped into his head. 'Down at the rest house? When the caretaker happened to mention you?'

'He doesn't normally mention me,' Shiva said softly. 'Unless I put the thought into his head.'

'Ah!' Adi said, grasping the implication. Shiva kept walking at a steady slow pace.

'I am mystified,' Adi said after a while, a bit sheepishly. 'How do you put thoughts into people's heads across such distances?'

'Oh, not very mysterious once you grasp the science behind it,' said Shiva.

'Will you explain that to me, Shiva?'

'Yes, I will. We have the whole night with us.' He looked at Adi with a twinkle in his eye.

'Why did you want me to come?' Adi asked. 'I mean, why did you put the thought into my head?'

'Haven't you always wanted to meet a yogi?' Shiva asked.

'Oh yes, since I was in school. My father used to talk a lot about yogis! But I could never find a real one.'

'So, here you are!'

'Have you known this about me since I was a kid?'

'No. Only when you entered my field of consciousness.'

'And when was that?'

'When you started your climb from Saung.'

'Your field of consciousness extends all the way to Saung?'

'Yes, when I'm in a less expansive mood.' Shiva chuckled softly.

'Whoa, that's amazing! And what happens when you are in a more expansive mood?'

He laughed. 'Depends on a lot of things. Moving parts…'

They had come very close to the stream now. The stream was sparkling playfully, and Adi could feel a fine mist around him. He stood quietly watching the stream. Shiva did not disturb his quietude.

'This is beautiful, Shiva…' Adi murmured after a long time.

'Yes,' Shiva whispered. 'When you are quiet, everything becomes beautiful.'

Adi stood there, watching the sparkling stream, and breathing in the cold night air, completely at peace. No question troubled his mind, no thought arose. Everything seemed to have disappeared into the mist that had enveloped him. After what seemed a very long time, a single thought arose in his mind—*Can I not always be in this kind of silence?*

Almost immediately, another thought came floating into his mind—*Sense the silence around you, Adi. This silence is the background of everything, even of your own mind and all its activities.*

'Did you just speak?' Adi turned sharply to Shiva. 'I heard your voice.'

'No, you didn't.' Shiva said. 'You received a thought. It sounded like my voice because it came from me, in response to your earlier thought.'

'Telepathy?' Adi couldn't keep the eagerness out of his voice.

'Kind of.'

'No, please—what was that?' Adi persisted. 'You read my mind and answered to my mind which I heard in my head, as distinctly as if you were speaking to me.'

'Telepathy means one mind communicating directly with another.'

Adi nodded.

'But the fact is,' Shiva continued, 'there are no two minds, no two consciousnesses.'

Adi focused on what Shiva was explaining. *No two minds?*

'In reality, there is only consciousness, one being. Think of it as a kind of cosmic mind. When your own mind becomes very quiet, the boundaries between minds dissolve, and that is when you realize that there is only one consciousness functioning as cosmic mind.'

A glimmer of understanding dawned.

'So, it is one mind in two places? Like two waves rising in the same ocean but in two different locations.'

'Not exactly. You want it as it is?'

This piqued Adi's curiosity even more. 'Of course!'

'There are no two locations,' said Shiva, almost conspiratorially. '*No two persons*. Everything is one, one single thing. It is not telepathy; it is more like non-locality!'

There was silence again, and the sound of the rushing stream. It was getting colder. Adi shivered involuntarily.

'Want to go back in?' Shiva asked. 'Must be pretty cold for you?'

Adi nodded. 'Yes, it is cold, in spite of all the layers I'm wearing.' Adi looked at Shiva's almost bare body. 'How do you manage? Yoga?'

'Since the identification, this body no longer feels the elements—cold, heat, rain, nothing makes much of a difference.'

'The body does not feel the elements, or is it mind over matter kind of a thing?'

'Well, the body is a sensing organ, so of course it senses the cold, but the consciousness is identified with Shiva, and not the body or the senses, and Shiva is beyond nature and her elements.'

'Your consciousness is identified with Shiva—that's what you said, right?'

'Yes, that is so,' Shiva replied.

'In other words,' Adi said pensively, 'for all practical purposes, you *are* Shiva, aren't you?'

'A bit more complicated than that,' Shiva said. 'For all practical purposes, everyone is Shiva, because the consciousness in all beings is one, and that one consciousness is Shiva. You understand?'

Adi nodded. 'This is the Vedanta philosophy, right?'

'Yes, that is right.'

'I thought Vedanta philosophy was just that—philosophy. Can it be experienced?'

'Vedanta is not speculative philosophy, young man. The rishis who spoke of it first realized it in themselves, experienced and validated it all, and only then spoke of it. Everything they said is based on lived reality—scientific and supremely logical.'

Shiva started walking back towards the house. Adi followed, lost in thought. *Studying philosophy is one thing*, he thought, *but getting it straight from someone who is living it is quite another*.

'So, there is a logic behind all this?' Adi asked.

'There is a logic behind everything,' Shiva said. 'But, of course, it is not the simple, linear logic your mind is used to. To grasp the nature of Shiva, you need a logic that goes beyond mind, a *supramental* logic, if you will.'

'You must have studied a lot!' Adi asked, impressed.

'Oh no, not really. I came up to the mountains when I was very young. I never went to any university.'

'But you speak so well, Shiva. Your English is so good!'

Shiva laughed. 'Don't get deceived, young man. I am using *your* mind to speak to *you*. It is your own English that you are hearing.'

Suddenly it struck Adi—*yes, he was right, the same accent, the same diction. Huh!*

'Because you think in English, Adi,' Shiva explained after a while. 'If you were thinking in Hindi or French, I would be speaking to you in Hindi or French!'

'Wow, this is beyond me! If I didn't know English, or think in it, you wouldn't know it either?'

'No, I wouldn't. I don't know a language till I need to use it.'

It took a moment for that to sink.

'What is *your* language, Shiva? What language do *you* think in?'

'I don't think at all!' Shiva said, simply and quietly. 'I haven't, for years.'

'You haven't thought for years?'

'My head is utterly empty. I don't have a language of my own.'

'So, right now you're speaking in English to me by using my own mind and its language?' Adi sounded completely flabbergasted.

'Yes.'

'And if I were thinking in French, you would be speaking to me in French?'

'Yes, indeed. Or any language in the world, modern or ancient.'

'This is incredible, Shiva.' Adi felt totally out of depth, almost as if he was in the presence of an extraterrestrial.

'You'll need to slow down, Adi. We have a whole night before us.'

Suddenly, out of the corner of his eye, Adi saw a looming shape at a distance, something that looked like a temple.

'What's that?' he asked, pointing to the structure. 'The temple?'

'Yes,' Shiva replied. 'No one ever goes there now.'

'I saw that temple in my dream. Twice.'

'Yes, I know that.'

'Did you have anything to do with that dream?'

'Of course!'

'What?'

'To bring you here.'

'Bring me here? But why?'

'Because you wanted to be here…'

'I wanted to be here? No, I didn't…before the dream, I didn't even know this temple existed!'

'Of course, you did.'

Adi stopped and looked at Shiva. 'You mean in some other lifetime?'

'You can say that.'

'Please, Babaji…Shiva…tell me what this is all about…'

'Tomorrow.'

'Tomorrow?'

'It's pretty late tonight…'

'My friends—'

Adi thought of Ira waiting for his return, but Shiva interrupted gently. 'I told you that it's taken care of. They will be waiting when you get back.'

'Taken care of?' *By some occult yogic process*, thought Adi to himself.

Shiva looked at Adi and smiled, Adi smiled back. It was liberating to be in the presence of someone you didn't have to hide anything from, not even your thoughts. You could just let go, like in a dream.

They got back to the cottage in a few minutes. Somehow it seemed that it took them a lot less time to come back. The warmth of the cottage was welcome. Shiva brought some blankets and placed them in front of Adi. 'This will make it a bit warmer for the night.'

'And we talk tomorrow?' Adi asked.

'Yes, tomorrow!' Shiva smiled at Adi, his eyes deep with mystery that Adi could not fathom. Adi wanted to think of Ira, and their trekking companions, but somehow couldn't. The thoughts wouldn't hold. Everything seemed to fade off into nothingness.

And then, deep sleep.

Shiva

'I want to learn yoga,' Adi said quietly, looking directly at Shiva. 'The science behind the Vedanta.'

Shiva was quiet for a while. The sound of crackling fire filled the room. It was deafeningly quiet outside. 'It is an exacting discipline, Adi,' he spoke at last, a bit grave. 'And once you come to it, there's no going back.'

'But there's a reason why I am here tonight, Shiva. This I understand—that I couldn't have come up here if you had not wanted me to. People don't come up here not because they don't want to but because they cannot, you don't allow them. I can see that much!'

'Yes, I know that you can see that. And you're right, there's a reason for your being here tonight. So far, it has been the force of destiny. You were destined to come here, Adi, even before you dreamed of the old temple. But now, you must make a conscious choice and commitment.'

Adi kept quiet.

'Or else, you can always turn back,' Shiva continued. 'You're young and you have a whole life before you. And you're intelligent, talented, articulate. You can achieve much in the world.'

'Shiva, I know that you know my future and what choice I will make.'

'No, Adi, I don't,' said Shiva earnestly. 'It doesn't work like that. If I knew your choice before you made it, then it wouldn't be free choice, would it?'

'So, it *is* free choice?'

'Absolutely!'

'And so, there *is* free will?'

'Yes, of course. The universe would be meaningless without free will. But free will comes only at critical turning points.'

'Like?'

'Like now.' Shiva smiled.

The words sank in. Adi sat still, his eyes closed, fully aware that he was at a tipping point in his life. If he chose to go back now, he would probably never come this way again. But if he chose to stay, whatever that meant, he could never go back to the world as he knew it, to his family, friends, his studies, his future...and to Ira. And as he thought of Ira, he felt a deep ache in his being, something he couldn't fathom.

Adi opened his eyes and looked at Shiva. He was sitting still, his eyes closed, even his breathing slowed to bare minimum. Only the shadows of the flames danced on the stone walls behind him. And then, suddenly, Adi felt a tremendous need to go the old temple. Somehow, he knew he was meant to, that it was the key to his future.

'Shiva!' Adi whispered, careful not to disturb Shiva's silence.

Shiva opened his eyes and looked at Adi. Something in Adi's heart burst open. For no reason, just like that, he felt a surge of joy, of sheer delight, rise from the base of his spine and shoot right up to his head, shaking his whole body as it went. Adi's head felt incredibly light after that—as if he had downed six drinks of rum at one go.

'Yes, Adi?' Shiva asked ever so gently.

'I want to go to the old temple, the one I saw in my dreams.'

'That temple is in ruins, no one has gone there for years. You will find bats, and maybe some wild animals.'

'I saw a person there…not too distinct, just a silhouette… tall, imposing.'

'Yes, a temple priest. I used to be that, once upon a time.'

'Once upon a time?'

'Many years ago, Adi—more years than you can possibly imagine.'

'A hundred, two hundred…?'

Shiva smiled. 'Four hundred, give or take.'

'Four hundred?' Adi stared disbelievingly at Shiva. Something was wrong here. Either Shiva was joking, or he was actually mad, or—

Once again, he couldn't complete his thought.

'Difficult to believe?' Shiva asked gently.

'Of course! If you were a temple priest four hundred years ago, how old would that make you?'

'How old do you think I am?' Shiva asked, with an amused smile.

'If I believe the caretaker down in Phurkia, I will say 120? Or 150? Beyond that—I don't think it is physically possible.'

'Physically—perhaps not. But is that all that we are?'

Adi looked hard at Shiva. His mind was utterly blank.

'We are not just physical bodies, Adi,' continued Shiva quietly. 'If you look deep enough into the physical body, into matter itself, you will see that we are pure consciousness, atman.'

'But mind is also consciousness, isn't it? Is there a difference between mind and atman?'

'Yes, mind is consciousness, but filtered through the senses, intellect, memory and ego. It is not pure. Atman is pure consciousness, not filtered through anything at all—no matter, no senses, no mind.'

'So, how does one know it then?'

'That's the thing, Adi—the atman cannot be known because the atman is the only knower.'

'And the knower cannot be known?' Adi recalled the central tenet of Vedantic epistemology.

'Who is there to know the knower? You see, for the knower to be known, it must become an object to itself, and that is not possible.'

'Yes,' Adi nodded. 'That is right. I can only know something when it is outside of me, an object to myself.'

'That is so,' Shiva said. 'But you, the one who wants to know all this, is the knower.'

'And I am the atman?'

'Yes, you are the atman.'

'But isn't it the buddhi—the intelligence—and not the atman, that wants to know all this?'

'Yes, all questions arise from the buddhi and its interaction with the universe. But you are not buddhi, just as you are not body and the senses, the mind or ego. You are atman, the one that shines through the senses, the mind, buddhi and ego.'

Adi touched his own hand. 'But this is physical, Shiva—I *am* this physical, material body too, am I not?'

'No, Adi,' Shiva said. 'Think about it. You are touching and feeling the body. In other words, you are aware of the body, the body is an object of your awareness, right?'

Adi nodded. 'Yes, that's right!'

'So, if you are aware of the body, are you the body or the awareness of the body?'

'Can I not be both?'

'Can there be a body without awareness of body?'

Adi thought for a moment. 'No, that would be a dead body.'

'Think about it: in deep sleep, or in deep meditation, the awareness of the body is gone, and so, for all practical purposes, the body is gone. Or, at least, become irrelevant.'

'In deep sleep, yes; I haven't experienced deep meditation, of course.'

'But when the awareness of the body is absent, is the awareness itself present?'

'Yes, I suppose so. While sleeping and dreaming, there is the dreamer-awareness.'

'The object of awareness may keep changing but the awareness will be there. For instance, when you are not aware of the body, you may be aware of the mind and its activities.'

'Yes, that often happens.'

'So the mind then becomes the object of awareness, right?'

'Yes, right. There are times I am aware of thought but not so much of the body.'

'But whether you are aware of the body and its sensations, or mind and its activities, does the awareness itself change from one to the other?'

Adi thought again. 'No,' he said after a while, 'it does not. Whatever be the object, the awareness itself does not change.'

'So, I ask again Adi, are you the awareness or the ever-shifting, ever-changing objects of awareness?'

'If I were the objects of awareness, I would myself keep changing and shifting, it is obvious therefore that I am the unchanging awareness behind the shifting objects.'

'Excellent!' Shiva remarked, his eyes lighting up. 'This is the first step towards self-realization—identifying with the awareness and not with the objects of awareness.'

Understanding dawned. 'This awareness that I am, this is the pure, unfiltered consciousness that you were speaking of, right? The atman?' Adi asked.

'Slow down, Adi,' Shiva said, smiling. 'The atman is a shoreless ocean. By realizing you are awareness and not its objects, you have just stepped onto the shore. You will now have to walk into the ocean, and then keep going…'

'And when will I realize the atman?'

'Realization of the atman is not a one-time event, Adi. It is an ongoing process, an infinite unfolding.'

Adi grew silent, reflecting on what he had just heard and understood. After a long pause, he looked up at Shiva. 'I understand now, Shiva. You have realized yourself as atman and no longer identify with the body. Since atman is pure consciousness, it can also be called Shiva, for Shiva is pure consciousness. And that is why you now call yourself Shiva—am I right in my understanding?'

Shiva seemed happy. 'Yes, you have the understanding. But I can sense questions too hiding in the background!'

'Yes, there are questions,' Adi said thoughtfully. 'I can understand that identifying with atman liberates you from the conditions and limitations of the body, but the body is still there, still very biological, still subject to age, degeneration, death. Or am I missing something here?'

'No, you are right. The body is still mortal, but its mortality is somewhat transformed by the power of the atman. You see, the atman is not just pure consciousness but also infinite force. Our ancients called it *chitshakti*—consciousness-force. *Chit*, as you know, is consciousness and *shakti* is force. But that is not all. There's more.' Shiva paused.

Adi waited patiently, assimilating all the information.

'Our Upanishads declare that the atman is brahman, the supreme being, the source of all becoming. This atman is brahman, there is no difference—*ayam atma brahman*, as the rishis said.'

'That is pure Vedanta. If I am atman, then I am brahman too. I am all there is, or ever can be!'

'Yes,' said Shiva. 'And as atman or brahman, your attributes are *sat, chit and ananda*—sat is reality, or existence itself, absolute being. Chit is absolute consciousness. Ananda is pure, infinite bliss. So, brahman is also satchidananda. And that is what the atman is, that is what you are!'

'It makes literal sense, Shiva, but totally beyond my comprehension. Absolute being and consciousness?'

'Absolute because there is no other existence or consciousness besides this. This is the one sole existence and one sole consciousness, pun entirely intended! We call it *ekam sat*—one truth, one reality, one being, one consciousness.'

'And the atman is this ekam sat?'

'Yes, and that is why we say that atman alone exists, and all else in existence are derivatives, transformations and formations of this one atman.'

Adi nodded slowly as the mystery cleared. 'So, is this what you have realized, Shiva, absolute being?'

'Yes, Adi. I have realized that I am that one, sole existence, ekam sat.' Shiva's tone was quiet and matter of fact.

Adi was looking closely at Shiva. What he was seeing was a somewhat imposing, elderly man with a lot of love and laughter in his eyes and deep tenderness on his face. His face was like a woman's—soft, tender, beautiful. But what he was hearing from him was quite beyond any human experience.

Am I, at this very moment, looking at absolute existence, absolute being?

Shiva apparently sensed his unspoken thought. 'It does sound strange, doesn't it? When you put it like that?'

'That I am, right now, in a fully waking state, looking at pure consciousness and absolute being?'

'Yes,' said Shiva with a chuckle.

'Who are you?' Adi asked, narrowing his eyes, with a quiet intensity in his voice. 'Are you Shiva?'

This better be real.

'Yes,' said Shiva, simply and unaffectedly, like a child. 'I am Shiva.'

'*The* Shiva?' asked Adi again.

'You mean your Mahadeva? Supreme God?'

Adi nodded, unable to say anything, dreading the answer.

Shiva continued nonchalantly,' If by Shiva you mean pure consciousness, absolute being and infinite delight of becoming, then yes, I know I am Shiva. But then, I also know you are Shiva. And so is every embodied conscious being in this universe. There can be no other consciousness besides Shiva and there can be no other being besides Shiva. Shiva is all there is.'

'But I don't know this as a fact, as you do,' said Adi. 'I haven't realized myself as Shiva, as you have!'

'That is true, Adi,' Shiva said softly, quietly. 'That is the only difference between us—I know I am Shiva, you don't. You still believe you are Adi, the person, the one who was born as Adi and will live his whole life as Adi.'

'But you were also born as somebody, weren't you? And you too will live your whole life as that somebody? So what if you now call yourself Shiva?' What's in a name?'

Adi was somewhat surprised by his own subtle aggressiveness. But he needed to get it right. Shiva simply smiled.

'Adi, I am not a somebody or anybody,' Shiva explained. 'I am not a person—I have no identity, no form, no name. I am identified only with Shiva, pure consciousness and being. Nothing moves in me but Shiva. Nothing thinks or wills or acts in me but Shiva. Do you understand?'

Adi continued looking at Shiva with growing fascination. 'Yes, I am beginning to get it. What I am looking at is the outer form—the body—of Shiva himself!'

'Yes,' Shiva said. 'But it's not as dramatic and unique as it sounds. You too are exactly the same—a namarupa of Shiva, like I am. Everyone, everywhere, is a namarupa of Shiva—the only difference is that I know it and you don't. When you look at me, you see and experience an individual, a person with a definite personality, character, identity, and when I look at you, I see no one else but Shiva.'

'But I do have a personality, character, identity—don't I?'

'An ocean has waves of all kinds. You can see the waves and get taken in by them, or you can keep your attention on the ocean and not get distracted by the waves.'

'The ocean is Shiva...' Adi began.

'And the waves are prakriti.' Shiva completed.

'And the waves have no value?' Adi asked.

'Oh, they do,' Shiva replied. 'But only as waves of the ocean.'

'Ah, I see!' A few minutes of complete silence passed. 'I am beginning to understand who you are, Shiva!'

Adi bowed low to Shiva. 'My pranam to Shiva that lives and manifests through you!'

Shiva also bowed low to Adi. 'And my pranam to Shiva who lives and manifests through you, Adi.'

≈

The fire was filling the room with its dancing flames and warmth. Shiva was sitting quietly on his rug in front of the fire, his eyes closed. Adi sat quietly before him, his mind still active with questions but his spirit calmer with the glow of a new understanding.

'I understand *sat* and *chit*, Shiva,' Adi spoke softly, not wanting to disturb the silence in the room. 'But *ananda* seems to escape me. Is ananda happiness, joy?'

Shiva opened his eyes and looked at Adi for a long time.

'I cannot explain ananda, Adi,' he said finally. 'You realize ananda when you realize sat-chit. Think of ananda as the very substance of existence and consciousness. To exist is to be conscious, to be conscious is to know ananda. Ananda is the infinite delight of the supreme identification, the self-becoming of Shiva. This ananda is the infinite bliss of being, the source of being and becoming, and the final dissolution of being. The seers say that from ananda all being arises, by ananda is all being and becoming sustained, and into ananda all being dissolves.'

'So, this obviously is not the human idea or experience of bliss or happiness!'

'No, this is not the happiness of the mind, body or senses, it is the infinite bliss of the atman and the realization of the atman. None can know this divine delight without first coming to the consciousness of atman.'

'How shall we realize this atman, and the divine delight of this atman, Shiva?' Adi asked. 'I am restless now...the understanding has lit a fire in me.'

'That is the agni of the atman's aspiration for itself, Adi. Give all you are, all you do, and all you have, to this agni, and let this agni grow ever brighter and higher in you. Cease from all other activities and give yourself completely to the contemplation of Atman.'

Adi closed his eyes. He could feel the echo of Shiva's words, like an ancient mantra, sink deep into his mind and heart. And then, out of his depths, as if aroused by the mantra, wave after wave of luminous understanding arose, tearing through veils of ignorance and delusion, entering the limbs and pores of his body, and sinking deeper and deeper into the very core of the matter that Adi's body was.

He saw luminous swirling energy, sometimes blue and sometimes white with golden bands, enter the very cells of his body, filling them up like living fluid. He felt his body, or the sense of his body, expanding, becoming ever vaster, moving out into the universe, spreading away into the farthest reaches of space. And then he saw the stars erupting in the depths of space, each star a ball of fire rising from some unknown and unfathomable depth of being.

And then he heard Shiva's voice resonating deep in his own consciousness.

'All matter is one, Adi. Know that. Whether what you call your body lives for forty years or four hundred, matters little. What matters is the atman, the consciousness, you infuse into the cells of the body, for by consciousness each cell becomes a living pulsation in the very fabric of spacetime. And thus, you grow into the universe and the universe grows into you. This is the meaning of Shiva's manifestation as matter and life, as cosmos, as earth.'

The Temple and the Inner Chamber

Adi opened his eyes slowly, as if awaking from a sleep of centuries. Everything seemed to be enveloped in a silvery mist. He closed his eyes again. Was he still dreaming? But he could hear a slow and steady drumbeat somewhere in the distance. It reminded him of heartbeats, but much louder. And then he heard bells ringing. He forced his eyes open and saw that the mist had cleared. He was standing on a stony platform under a huge tree. Right before him was the ancient rock-hewn temple of his dreams. But this was not a dream. The stony platform under his feet felt solid, and cold. He looked down. He was barefoot. No wonder the ground felt so cold. He also felt the cold on his skin. He suddenly shivered when he realized that his upper body was bare, like a brahmin's. He looked up at the temple before him. It was exactly as he had seen it in his dream. A few stony steps led up to a small wooden door opening into the temple.

He climbed the steps and came up to the door. He bent low and peered inside. There was a glow coming from deeper within the temple. And there was a strong sweet fragrance wafting out from the inside of the temple. Still bending low, he entered the temple slowly and guardedly. Once inside, he straightened up. It was cool inside the temple.

He then saw another wooden door, somewhat higher than the main door, leading to a smaller room inside. He walked through that door into the inner room. The room was circular, with a black marble Shivalinga right in the middle. There were a few rugs arranged on the floor, circling the linga. Shiva was sitting on one of them, facing him, his eyes closed, his body erect, hands on his knees. He seemed not to be breathing at all, so still was his body. Adi sat down carefully on one of the rugs, facing Shiva. Then he too closed his eyes, bringing his awareness to his breathing.

It was then that he noticed that it was completely silent and still inside, no drumbeat, no bell, no movement. He could just hear his own heartbeats. Adi had never experienced such total silence before, a silence that seemed to hang physically in the air of the inner chamber.

≈

He suddenly felt that Shiva was looking at him, and the feeling was so distinct that he opened his eyes. Shiva was indeed looking straight at him, a light smile playing about his lips. He looked taller and broader in the dull glow around him. He also looked a lot younger. Adi joined his palms and bowed his head to Shiva. Shiva nodded.

'So, you are in your temple at last, Adi!' Shiva seemed to be speaking directly into Adi's head. The silence of the chamber remained unbroken.

'Thank you,' Adi said quietly. He was somewhat taken aback when he couldn't hear himself speaking. 'I couldn't have come here without you.'

'Do you recognize the temple?' Shiva asked.

'Yes,' Adi replied, 'the one I dreamed of, except that this one doesn't look so old or dilapidated!'

'It isn't,' Shiva stated simply. 'What you saw in your dream was this temple about four hundred years in the future.'

'You mean we are four hundred years in the past right now?'

'More or less!'

Adi looked at Shiva, then at himself, completely baffled. 'Hypnosis? Mental projection?'

Shiva said nothing in response. He kept looking, somewhat amused, at Adi.

'None of this is real, is it?' Adi asked after a while. 'Please tell me.'

'No, it is not real. But it is not illusion either,' Shiva spoke slowly, deliberately.

'Neither real nor illusion?'

'You and I have both been here, in this temple, those many years ago. I was the head priest, and you were my apprentice.'

'I came to train as a priest?'

'Yes, and you were very good! An exemplary Shiva devotee! You were having deep spiritual experiences even as a young apprentice. You were extraordinary, one of my best students!'

Shiva was smiling fondly as he reminisced. Adi, despite himself, and though he remembered nothing, was feeling a sense of pride. He still couldn't relate to what was unfolding before him, but he could not doubt Shiva's words either.

'What happened then? I remember nothing, of course!' Adi said.

'Oh, I taught you the mahavidyas related to Shiva and Shakti, and you absorbed them all, like a sponge. You also learnt the mantra-shastras and the tantras!'

'I have no idea what these things are,' Adi said. 'Seems the forgetting is complete.'

'*Nothing* is ever forgotten, Adi, *nothing* is completely lost.'

'Then how come I do not even know what these things are?'

'Your buddhi in this incarnation does not know because it is veiled by the maya of time. But your atman does, for the atman forgets nothing, loses nothing. It preserves the most conscious part of your existence, to unfold it again, in some other life, some other form.'

'I thought the atman is universal, one atman, one being.'

'So it is, but that does not mean that it cannot retain an essence of the personal. The personal-universal duality is a mind construct, it has no meaning in the consciousness of the atman.'

'Hmm, so if I can reach deep enough into myself, I will touch the atman, and remember everything?'

'Once you strip away the external layers of mind and personality, the various veils of ahankara, you will know yourself as atman, and you will remember all that is worth remembering.'

'Worth remembering?'

'From the perspective of spiritual evolution, Adi. Only experiences and realizations that have spiritual value are kept in the memory of the atman. I say *memory* because in English we don't have a better expression. What the atman preserves is samskara—seeds of future realizations and experiences. All our lifetimes and karmic destinies spring forth from these seeds.'

'Ah, I understand. Obviously, there's no use retaining memories of all experiences. Most of our ordinary experiences are forgettable, anyway!'

'That is so,' Shiva said. 'What the atman in us chooses to remember of one life is what is carried forth as seed to the next.'

'So, how do I make sure that my atman chooses to remember a particular experience?'

'Bring the atman to the front of your being, replace the psychological self—the chitta, buddhi, ahankara—with the atman. Then the atman will choose.'

'The atman can choose? Is not choice a mental thing?'

'There is no mental thing, Adi. Behind all the powers, capacities and faculties of the mind is the single power and light of the atman. Find the atman and all this shall be revealed to you.'

'And you, Shiva, have realized the atman, and therefore you remember all this?'

'The atman knows, yes.'

'You remember all your past lives, Shiva?'

'Time, as past, present and future, does not exist in the consciousness of the atman. So, there is no remembrance, only an unbroken perception of all time, of all lives. We call it *trikala jnana*—unbroken knowledge of all time, of all events, all causes and effects.'

'And you have the trikala jnana?'

'He who lives in Shiva possesses the trikala jnana. In fact, Shiva is Mahakala, that which transcends all of time, space and existence.'

'And you are identified with Shiva, who is Mahakala, who is Mahadeva?'

'We use multiple names and descriptions for the one true being that Shiva is. When you know him in your heart, you don't need any names or descriptions for him. You pass into his silence, for that is where he reveals himself to you.'

'What knowledge remains then, in that silence? What indeed is the mark of that identification? How does one know?'

'*Mano buddhi ahankara chittani naaham…*' Shiva intoned in the silence, the words ringing clear through Adi's consciousness. '*Na cha shrotra jihve na cha ghraana netre, na cha vyoma bhumir na tejo na vaayuhu, chidananda rupah shivoham shivoham…*'

'I am not mind, nor intellect, nor thought nor ego…' Adi's mind was repeating in English to itself. 'I am neither the senses nor ether, earth, fire or air, I am the Self of Eternal Bliss, Shiva am I…'

'*Shivoham, shivoham…*' Shiva continued intoning the seed mantra for invoking Shiva in oneself.

The mantric incantation reverberated through the dome of the chamber, getting louder and louder, drowning Shiva and Adi as they sat facing each other in the dim glow of light. Centuries seemed to dissolve in their consciousness, and all time collapsed into a single luminous flash of knowing, being and becoming. A lightning flash that was not of time or space but of pure consciousness.

≈

Adi was wearing an ochre robe, his head clean-shaven, like a monk's, and the outline of an eye drawn on his forehead in sandalwood. He stood tall and straight, looking out at some unknown object in the distant horizon. Shiva quietly walked up to him and stood by his side, not wishing to disturb his contemplation. Minutes passed in silence and stillness.

'*Dhyanam kutra asti, vatsa*?' Shiva asked in Sanskrit.

Adi turned to face him, understanding the deeper implication of the question.

'*Shunyatayam*,' Adi replied in Sanskrit.

'Can one's dhyana be in emptiness?' Shiva asked, continuing in Sanskrit.

'Isn't dhyana itself empty?' Adi asked, continuing in Sanskrit too.

'Therefore, all things can be borne in dhyana,' Shiva said.

'And the dhyana,' Adi continued softly, 'is its own object. To become what one contemplates is the highest state of contemplation.'

'Have you become the object of your dhyana?' Shiva asked.

'Shiva is the object of my dhyana, Gurudev,' Adi replied.

'Then, the object is to become Shiva himself?' Shiva asked again.

'None can become Shiva, Gurudev,' Adi replied.

'Why is that so, Adi?' asked Shiva.

'This consciousness I am is Shiva!' Adi replied.

'Do you know the consciousness you are, Adi?' Shiva asked again.

'I know that I am, Gurudev.'

'And what is this world, Adi?' Shiva asked.

'It is but consciousness itself, Gurudev.'

'Is there no world then?' Shiva asked.

'There is, and there is not!' Adi replied.

'How is it there?' Shiva asked.

'For the consciousness becomes the world and assumes the namarupa of jagat.'

'And how is it not there?'

'When you know consciousness as consciousness, there is no jagat.'

'Yet people do perceive and experience jagat, don't they? Without knowing consciousness.'

'That is the delusion, Gurudev,' Adi said. 'To see the jagat as jagat and not as consciousness is avidya.'

'Whence does avidya arise, Adi?' Shiva asked.

'It is self-generated, Gurudev. It arises from itself, born of its own womb.'

'And how is it resolved, Adi?'

'By the illumination of jnana.'

'And what exactly is that jnana, Adi?' Shiva asked.

'*Tattva jnana*, Gurudev,' Adi replied. 'The knowledge that all that is manifest is Shiva, and all that is not manifest is Shiva; that Shiva arises from Shiva as its own Shakti, and Shakti manifests in turn as prakriti, and prakriti radiates out into manas, buddhi, chitta, ahankara, and these then form samsara. And all this, from samsara to prakriti, resolves into Shakti again, and Shakti is reabsorbed into Shiva as it must always, at the end of all cycles of being and becoming.'

'And how does one attain to that tattva jnana, Adi?' Shiva continued, relentless.

'By two things, Gurudev,' Adi replied, calm as ever. 'Dhyana and Shiva's Grace.'

'And what is the object of dhyana?' Shiva asked again, his voice intense and penetrating.

'Shiva himself.' Adi replied, his voice calm.

'How does one contemplate Shiva when one does not know Him?' Shiva asked.

'One can know Shiva by concentrating one's entire consciousness on itself, like a serpent swallowing its tail and disappearing into itself. No other kind of knowledge of Shiva is possible, for Shiva, being all there is—*sarvam Shiva mayam jagat*—Shiva is beyond all knowledge. There is none to know or realize Him, and thus is He known as the Unknowable, the Unmanifest, the Avyakta. Only by perfect identification can He be known.'

'*Shivoham, shivoham*,' Shiva intoned softly.

'*Shivoham shivoham*,' Adi repeated.

Nothing Dies

Adi opened his eyes and looked at Shiva sitting still before him, his body reflecting the glow of the chamber's light.

'What dies, Gurudev?' Adi asked quietly, still looking at Shiva's unmoving body.

'Nothing dies, Adi,' Shiva replied, without opening his eyes or forming words. 'Nothing is ever destroyed or created in this universe. What we see as death is just a change of phase for the atman. In its progression through lives and forms, the atman often changes phases and orders of existence. It discards old forms and expressions that are no longer needed to take on new ones.'

'But something does die!'

'The body, you mean? Or the person you call yourself?'

'Well, the body for sure.'

'The body is *jada*, inert, to begin with. It is the atman, by the *pranic* force, that animates it, makes it sentient. When atman chooses to pass on to its next phase of evolution, and is ready to discard the body, the prana withdraws from the body, and the body falls to ground. That is what people call death.'

'So, the body returns to the elements?'

'Yes, it returns to the elements, to molecules and atoms, and then to *akasha*, the subtle ether out of which space and time emerge, and all the subtle elements, emerge.'

'Tell me about this akasha, Gurudev.'

'We know of this akasha also as consciousness-space, chidakasha. Out of this infinite chidakasha, life and mind arise; and out of life and mind, ahankara arises. When the atman withdraws from the annamaya, the physical sheath, the ahankara, mind and life all dissolve back into chidakasha.'

'And this chidakasha is knowable to us?'

'Yes, for at the very core of your being is this chidakasha. Shiva himself is this infinite chidakasha, and knowing him, you will know all.'

'And what happens to the mind, Gurudev, when atman withdraws from the annamaya?' Adi asked.

'Nothing of the mind is ever lost either, Adi,' Shiva explained. 'What the mind experiences, realizes and understands are absorbed forever in its subtle substance as *prajna*, distilled wisdom. When the body falls off, the individual mind resolves into the cosmic mind, and its prajna is absorbed into chidakasha as *prakash*—illumination. Mind, in its essence, returns to *prakash* in the chidakasha. That is the loop, Adi.'

'What kind of illumination is prakash?' Adi asked.

'The illumination of consciousness, that which shines through the awakened and enlightened buddhi. This prakash is indestructible and remains preserved in chidakasha forever. Nothing, therefore, is lost, no understanding or true knowing is ever forgotten. What you, as Adi, have understood and realized individually will remain in the form of prakash in the chidakasha, to return, again, as knowledge and intuition to minds that will, through countless generations, thirst for understanding and enlightenment.'

'Thus, the universe itself grows towards consciousness and light?'

'Yes, Adi—out of Light it was born and into Light it must resolve.'

'So, body returns to akasha, mind to prakash. And what about *me*? The one that thinks, knows, feels, understands?'

'The psychological self, the ahankara, is an aggregate of memories, impressions, thoughts, feelings, tendencies, habits. And all of it falls apart when the atman withdraws. But we are not just the ahankara, are we?'

'No, we are the *purusha* behind the ahankara.'

'Yes, the *chaitya purusha*, the one who is conscious in our consciousness, the one who is awake in us while we sleep, who grows in us while we struggle and suffer, the one who is the knower within, the eternal presence through all our becomings.'

'And this, therefore, cannot be destroyed?'

'*Ajo nityah shashvato yam purano, na hanyate hanyamane sharire*...' Shiva chanted in Sanskrit.

'It is unborn, eternal, indestructible and timeless—it is not destroyed when the material body is destroyed—Krishna's great teaching to Arjuna?'

'Yes,' said Shiva, smiling. 'That which sets the tone for the whole of the Bhagavad Gita. One who grasps this, Adi, loses all fear and weakness and becomes stable in the highest wisdom!'

'But one first has to realize this indestructible atman, this eternal *chaitya purusha*?'

'And for that,' said Shiva, 'one has to turn to oneself, to one's inmost being, for there lies the key, the secret of secrets!'

'And, I suppose, it would be pointless to ask how?'

'The answer, dear Adi, is already known to you. All you need to do is still the waves of your mind, and everything will become transparent.'

Shiva was gazing deep into Adi's eyes, penetrating through the layers of his mind and ego, looking straight, as it were, into his very soul. Adi became still, his whole being transfixed by Shiva's penetrating gaze. Time ceased. All distances disappeared. The entire universe seemed gathered at a single point of being—radiant, infinitely calm—that was neither Adi nor Shiva.

≈

Adi felt his body dissolving into currents of electricity—*vidyut*. In a trice, he was pure mind, spreading in directions and dimensions that the mind itself could not map. Adi felt that he was everywhere at once, and knowledge from all directions was streaming into him. Wave upon wave of light entered his subtle being, turning him into a luminous disembodied understanding that only kept to itself a memory of personal form. He then felt the universe itself unfolding, like a flower in slow motion time-lapse photography, from complete emptiness to an incredibly intense glow of light, which then radiated outward at blinding speed, becoming billions of vortices of fire in the blink of an eye; and then the numberless vortices of fire dissolved into a single luminous point—*bindu*—of blinding intensity that entered deep into his being, falling into a bottomless abyss of pure light.

And then he knew that he was everything—the bindu, the intensities of light, the vortices of fire, the emptiness of space and the vast consciousness spreading across measureless dimensions. He knew, with the crystal clarity of direct experience, what he was, and what he was meant to become.

'I am Light,' he thought in that profoundest of silences—a thought that was sacred and singular. 'I am the source of this universe, the first-born of Shiva. From Me, all things have arisen, and into Me they will return. All things and beings are forms that I absorb into Myself as fire absorbs into itself its own sparks. There is no death in me, as there is no birth—I am that which is and always shall be. I am the measure of all things and yet I am the immeasurable; I am the sound in all syllables and yet I am the silence of the Unmanifest. I am Shiva myself, and I alone go forth into the infinite vastness of existence as His Shakti.'

And then he dissolved into that vast of being, and all that he was, and had become, in that mystical instant, returned to form and name, space and time. No memory of that instant remained, for no time-bound consciousness could retain that cosmic event or its cosmic memory. But a single luminous drop of that realization fell into the cosmic mind and was absorbed into the very fabric of space and time.

≈

When Adi opened his eyes again in the dim glow of the temple's chamber, Shiva was in deep trance, his body seated immobile before him, eyes closed. Adi slowed down his breath for he knew even *that* could cause a ripple of disturbance in Shiva's trance. Adi waited in that palpable silence of the inner chamber, his mind still absorbing the experience and understanding he had just been brought to. He now knew with complete clarity that there was no universe out there, that he himself was the universe that had, over billions of years, become self-conscious as Adi. He also knew that Adi was just a certain form and character, a namarupa, amongst billions of other such namarupas, of an infinitely existing and growing cosmos. The one seated before him, the one who called himself Shiva, the one he now recognized as his ancient Guru, was also the same cosmos, the same matter, the same growing self-consciousness. He now knew, in the very cells of his body, that cosmos and life and consciousness is one single being and one single becoming—seamlessly, endlessly, beyond all human measure.

Adi was inwardly awake now to his cosmic reality. He was still Adi, he felt it in his bones; but he also knew, simultaneously, that there was no Adi—what he was still feeling in his bones, in his inmost being, was not Adi at all but timeless existence itself, pure being. What the ancient Indian seers called *brahman*.

After what seemed like hours, Shiva opened his eyes, slowly emerging from his trance. He saw Adi sitting before him, an ethereal light of understanding on his face. Shiva understood at once what Adi had experienced and smiled. Adi smiled back, in profound gratitude. He knew there was no need for words any longer. There was no Shiva, no Adi. All was himself.

Tat twam asi, Adi heard Shiva in his mind—*that* thou art.

Aham brahmasmi, Adi uttered in his head, as if in response to Shiva's thought—I am that *brahman*.

'And yet,' Shiva whispered in Adi's mind, 'this is only the first immersion. There's an ocean beyond.'

'*An ocean beyond?*' Adi thought to himself. And the understanding came almost simultaneously with the thought. *The ocean is shoreless, boundless…there is no beginning, no end.*

'Where are you, O Shiva, in all this?' Adi directed his thought to Shiva in his mind. 'Have you realized this shoreless ocean?'

Adi felt his mind light up with Shiva's inward smile. 'This is the beauty and mystery of the shoreless ocean, Adi. The infinite cannot be portioned into finite measures. We are all at the same distance from all points of the infinite. We are all the same measure of the infinite. None is more, none is less; none is near, none is far. This ocean is measureless because it is beyond space and time, and all our human measures are of space and time.'

Adi understood at once. *But are there not measures of realization? But if being itself is infinite, how can there be measures of its realization? Any realization of being would be being, which then would be infinite. If one takes the infinite from the infinite, the infinite remains…*

Adi then heard Shiva's voice resonating deeply and quietly in his mind—*purnasya purnamadaya purnam evavashisyate.*

A Walk to the Stream

Adi stood up slowly, careful not to disturb the pure silence of the temple's chamber. There was something here that was far too precious and rare to be dissipated by human thought or movement. No wonder this temple did not allow anyone to come to it. Outwardly what may seem to be in ruins may inwardly still be pristine. But then, that is not for everyone to know—nature veils her secrets well.

Adi exited the temple into bright and crisp sunlight. The air was fresh and invigorating. He stretched his limbs like an animal that had just woken from hibernation. His skin absorbed the sunlight gratefully and blissfully. He walked to the edge of the stone platform on which the temple stood. Beyond the platform was open forest, and beyond the forest, a deep valley. He kept walking slowly, conscious of every step and movement, into the forest. The smell of pine was heavy in the air. In the far distance, he could hear the murmur of a stream.

Soon he came upon the stone cottage where he had met Shiva. He walked up the garden path into the patio of the cottage. He sat down on the wooden reclining chair on which he had sat when he first reached the cottage. It seemed an event in a very distant past. Maybe some other lifetime. He sank into the chair and sighed, closing his eyes, breathing lightly. He realized in a while that he was not thinking of anything at all, he was just listening, breathing, resting. Then he became aware that there was no thought in the mind, just the thought that there was no thought. Then even that thought disappeared, and there was silence.

Which was gently broken by Shiva's presence—calm, gentle, vast. Adi opened his eyes and smiled at Shiva. 'My deep gratitude, Shiva,' he said softly, as he stood up. 'For letting me into the temple.'

'You came for the temple, didn't you?' Shiva smiled back.

'Long ago, it seems,' Adi said, pensively. 'In some other life.'

'Yes, it is always like that—time is so relative.'

'Now I know why no one visits the temple. Everyone sees it as a ruin.'

'The temple is a metaphor, Adi, a metaphor in matter. One has to go behind the metaphor to experience the temple. Which you did.'

'And I met my Guru,' Adi said, smiling at Shiva, a grateful, happy smile.

Shiva looked carefully at Adi for a few seconds. 'You saw a reflection, Adi,' he said after a while. 'The guru does not reside anywhere in space or time, he is always with you, but behind a veil of consciousness. When the veil falls, you see the reflection in your own consciousness. That which you always were.'

Adi understood this immediately. In fact, in the mind's silence, he *saw* exactly what Shiva was explaining. 'This is a new thing,' Adi said. 'The understanding comes without thought, without reasoning. Like it was always there, and the moment you articulate it, I see it shining within.'

'That is the true understanding. It is always there, in the consciousness. You don't need to get at it through any reasoning or meditation. Someone just has to light it up for you.'

'Yes, that is what the Guru does—illumines what we have within.'

'Let's go for a walk, Adi,' Shiva suggested. 'You've been sitting for quite a while.'

'Sure,' Adi instantly agreed. 'That would be nice.'

'Would it be *nice*?' Shiva asked, as they started walking into the garden. 'Or would it just be a walk?'

'Without thought,' Adi replied, 'it would just be a walk, neither nice nor not nice. I said it out of old habit.'

'The problem is with the language,' Shiva said, as they strolled down the garden path. 'We project our thoughts and states onto reality—nice, not nice, cold, warm, good, bad, necessary, unnecessary, and all that. If thought were to cease, there would be no such qualifiers to things that simply are or happen. Like this walk. It's just happening, an event in spacetime. And through this event, the entire universe is unfolding. This is how it always is.'

Adi understood exactly what Shiva meant. His mind was still very quiet, simply listening, aware of its own movement, its own habits and conditionings. Everything was clear as crystal, no veil, no justification, no explanation.

'It is getting colder,' Adi observed quietly, as if continuing Shiva's thought. 'Which is simply a sensation in the body with no correspondence in the consciousness.'

'The consciousness,' Shiva said, 'does not feel hot or cold. And for the body, it is just sensation, neither pleasant nor unpleasant.'

'Until one calls it one or the other. And when the mind is quiet, there is no label, description or qualifier.'

Shiva nodded, and they continued walking in silence. The sound of the stream grew louder as they came closer to it. Adi looked in the direction of the old temple and saw it again—an abandoned, dilapidated structure in the jungle. He smiled to himself. *How little we see, how little we know!*

'Because the consciousness in us is wrapped up in small, petty things,' Shiva said, picking up Adi's thought. 'We need to stretch the consciousness of the world, make it grow wider, more and more oceanic…'

'By stretching our own consciousness?'

'Is there another way?' Shiva asked quietly.

'Oceanic is the exact opposite of what most people are.'

'That may well be so. But keep Shiva always in the heart, try always to bring down his vastness into this world. That is the key to the yoga. Knowing Shiva, identifying with Shiva, is only the first step of the great yoga.'

'And the next step, Shiva?'

'To call down Shiva into the very substance of our world. That would indeed be yoga—union, oneness.'

'Yes, that seems to be the only true work, the karma and the yoga.'

'This yoga of expanding, becoming more and more oceanic, is to be done in the depths of our consciousness, quietly and humbly, step by step, stage by stage, till everything in us has outgrown its pettiness, its stubborn smallness, its absurd identification with the trivial and the ephemeral.'

'And the end? What will be the fulfilment of this great yoga?'

'To know, even in our bodies, that we are all children of immortality—*amritasya putrah*—is to know the Shiva in us, for Shiva is that pure, immortal consciousness in all existence. And that, Adi, is the peak of all we can ever know or realize—and that would be the fulfilment. *Purnata*.'

'Shivoham is the siddhi, the final identification, when all our being identifies with that which is the pure, eternal Self in us.'

'Shivoham in the mind, the heart, the limbs and cells of the body, in intention, thought, speech and action—integrally, Adi, top to bottom, shivoham, shivoham. That would be the siddhi of the great yoga.'

'How did this yoga come to you, Shiva?'

Shiva smiled. 'It was a long time ago...I no longer remember it all, nor do I care to.'

'Do you remember your name before identifying with Shiva?'

Shiva grinned. 'I had more than one, and none worth remembering.'

'But there is still an I, isn't there? Or is that a habit of language?"

'The I will always be there, Adi,' Shiva said. 'That is the whole point of self-consciousness. The I is not always *ahankara*, it is also *suddha ahambhav*, pure self-awareness.'

'But in the non-duality of Shiva-consciousness, where you and I no longer exist as separate selves, what would the "I" refer to?'

'To being itself, of course!'

They kept walking in silence till they reached the stream. The water was sparkling in the sunlight. They could hear all kinds of birds and insects. But the sounds blended perfectly with the quietude. Nothing was out of place, every movement and sound seamlessly woven.

'Do you remember what you were before the identification with Shiva?'

'That which was myself before the identification no longer exists, except as some irrelevant memories in the consciousness. And that which I now am identified with has no history, no biography, no existence in time.'

Adi and Shiva sat down on a boulder by the stream, and Shiva dipped his feet into the water. Adi too took off his shoes and put his feet into the water. He felt the pure sensation of cold water washing over his feet, and a shiver running up his spine. It felt good. But then, 'good' was a word, a thought, breaking the silence of the sensation. Sensations and feelings are silent, Adi realized, unlike thoughts and emotions.

When mind is silent, time ceases. There is no next moment, or the next thing to do, and so, there is no movement. The inner stillness merges with the stillness outside and all boundaries and separations dissolve. There is no person to experience this—the experience happens to itself, unfolding in an aloneness beyond human measure.

Another Night, Another Dimension

By the time Adi and Shiva got back to the ashram, it was late afternoon, the sun sinking quietly into the horizon, and a deep hue of orange spreading rapidly across the sky.

'I will make some tea for us,' Shiva declared.

'That would be wonderful,' Adi said warmly. And then, he thought about it. *What would be so wonderful about tea? It is, after all, a taste, a sensation.*

Shiva smiled. 'More than that, Adi,' he said. 'It is an emotional experience that mind builds around the simple act of having tea.'

'Yes, it is very satisfying, the simple act of sipping tea after a long walk in the cold. Though I know, even as I say all this, that there is no meaning in the words satisfying, long, cold…a walk is a walk. Simple.'

'You are deconstructing the human experience, Adi.' Shiva said lightly. 'You go on doing that while I make the tea.'

As Shiva disappeared into the cottage, Adi sat on the chair and took a deep breath. The orange and red hued sky looked beautiful. And as soon as he thought that, the thought fell apart—all that remained were the colours, the light breeze, the nip in the air. But it still felt good. There was a lightness in his being that he had never experienced before. This was not emotion, nor memory or imagination. It was a physical lightness, yet much more than just physical. As if his body, though seated in the reclining chair, was spread out, touching the sky, the colours, the breeze, even the sun, almost physically. Everything was vivid, throbbing with vitality, yet incredibly light.

And so was the tea. An incredible 'experience'. Reminded Adi of the dinner the night before. He had never had tea so invigorating before, anywhere.

'Do you put yogic force into your food and tea, Shiva?' Adi asked narrowing his eyes.

Shiva chuckled. 'You bet! Everything I touch becomes yogic!'

'No, seriously?' Adi persisted.

'Seriously,' Shiva responded. 'My whole being is in yoga with Shiva. So how can I touch or make anything without that consciousness which I call Shiva flow into it?'

Adi sipped the tea with far more awareness than before. This was no ordinary tea. For no reason, the thought of Ira and her friends waiting for him popped into his head. The thought of Phurkia, and the trek back. But then he smiled. *It's all taken care of,* he thought. *In Shiva's infinite consciousness!*

Shiva caught the thought and smiled back at Adi, quietly nodding. *It's all taken care of.*

The sun had set, and it was cold. But for the first time in Adi's experience, he was not *feeling* cold. The cold was just a thought in the mind, and that thought too dissolved as soon as he turned his attention to it. Only the pure physical sensation remained, no reaction rose in the mind. *Consciousness does not feel heat or cold.*

'Am I ready to learn yoga, O Shiva?' Adi asked after a long time in silence.

'Yes, Adi,' Shiva replied quietly. 'You are ripe for the yoga.'

'How long will it take to learn the yoga?' Adi asked.

'Learn the yoga? But the yoga is within you, Adi, though forgotten. You'll only have to bring it back to your consciousness.'

Adi thought of his experience in the temple. 'Some of it seems already to be coming back, Shiva.'

'Yes, I know. And all of it will come back too.'

'But that will take time, won't it?'

'Time is all relative, Adi. You know that by now. How long does it take for you to recall something you have forgotten?'

'Sometimes forever.'

Shiva kept looking at Adi closely.

'And sometimes in a flash, it's all there.'

Shiva smiled. 'And what do you do when you need to recall something?'

'Concentrate.'

Shiva nodded. 'Precisely. Just let the mental waves settle.'

'It took even the great seers many years of practice to come to the realization!'

'How would you know that, Adi?'

Adi thought for a while. No, there was no way he could know that. He had only heard or read about it.

'You see, this is a common error—the practice or sadhana is one thing, the realization is quite another. You may do lifetimes of sadhana, but the realization comes in a trice.'

'*Because* of the sadhana, isn't it?'

'No, not necessarily. Not always. There is no direct causal relationship between the effort and the realization. *Non sequitur*, as you philosophers would say.'

'But isn't the realization an outcome of the effort?'

'No.'

'Then?'

'Then what?'

'I mean, what brings it about?'

'Divine Grace.'

'Oh!'

After a long pause, Adi asked again, 'Is there a condition for the Grace to act?'

'No one, not even the greatest of yogis, can figure out divine Grace.'

'Is it arbitrary?'

'Of course not. It is supremely logical because it is divine—but divine logic is supracosmic and supramental.'

'So, where does that leave us?'

'You go on doing what you feel and believe is the best you can do. The Grace will do what it must, in its own way.'

'So, what did you do? Wait for the Grace?'

'No, I concentrated on quelling the waves of chitta. That was my only sadhana, let's say. *Yogaschittivritti nirodhah*—that was my only mantra, and it rose from within.'

'It rose from within?'

'Yes, and that,' Shiva winked, 'was divine Grace!'

Adi closed his eyes. He recalled the words of Rishi Patanjali, almost as if the Rishi himself was whispering in his mind—*yogaschittavritti nirodhah, tada drashtu svarupe avasthanam*. Yoga is the utter calming of consciousness, and when the consciousness is thus calmed, utterly stilled, the Self rests in its own being. *When the ripples of a lake are stilled, you can clearly see the bottom of the lake*.

'I understand.' Adi spoke softly, more to himself than to Shiva. 'My mind still has waves. I cannot yet see the bottom clearly.'

'Are you aware of these waves, Adi?'

'Yes,' Adi replied, watching his mind intently. 'Waves of all kinds, all colours, all shapes. Waves of desire, fear, aversion—some intense, some superficial. Preferences of all kinds, for this or that outcome, this should happen, this should not, this must, this must not, this is mine, that is not...and then memories, past and future, and images of all kinds...things I never think of...things long gone, long forgotten...'

'That is good, Adi, you are now witnessing your own mental play.'

Shiva leaned forward towards Adi. 'Let us try something,' he whispered. He reached out and touched Adi's forehead with his index and middle fingers, right between the eyebrows, the centre known to yogis as the *ajna-chakra*.

As soon as Adi felt Shiva's touch on his forehead, his eyes closed and all the waves and ripples faded away from his awareness, and all that remained was an endless calm, like a motionless sea extending in all directions.

≈

After what seemed ages, Adi became aware of ripples spreading across the motionless sea, ripples that slowly advanced towards him and entered his mind.

'I have given you Shiva's silence, Adi,' he heard Shiva's voice in his head. 'You have now stepped into the shoreless ocean of being. Let Shiva take you where you need to go. You have no further need of thought or knowledge. Om!'

When Adi opened his eyes, he saw Shiva sitting before him, smiling, completely at ease. His head was empty, the brain immobile. No ripple of thought broke the calm of his mind, no memory arose. All that he could sense of himself was a vastness of being, unmoving, immutable and everything else—the trees, the sound of the stream in the distance, the mountains, the sky above, even Shiva's body before him—seemed like distant images floating in the vastness. Adi kept concentrating on Shiva till all his consciousness became the very form of Shiva. In the language of the yogis, Adi's entire consciousness became a *Shiva-vritti*. The Shiva-vritti then rose like a tidal wave, inundating all that was felt and known, and then fell back into the vastness, disappearing into it, like a single ripple of water disappearing into the ocean.

When Adi returned to consciousness, after what seemed like ages, Shiva was standing beside him holding a cup of tea in his hand.

He smiled at Adi. 'You were in deep concentration, Adi!'

Adi smiled back. 'I'm getting to know you, old man!' He said with a twinkle in his eye. 'You can't play your hide and seek any more with me!'

'Hiding in plain sight, wouldn't you say?' There was a twinkle in Shiva's eye too.

Adi stared at Shiva, his eyes trying to penetrate a luminous veil. And then it dawned on him. Shiva is not out there, in some hidden dimension, avyakta and all that—he is always there, standing right before you, hiding nothing, veiling nothing. But we don't know what to look for, or even where to look. *Hiding in plain sight*. As he looked hard at Shiva, the man sitting before him on the ledge, he knew that he was not looking at Shiva at all, he was simply looking at a physical form, a reflection. Shiva cannot be seen or known, for Shiva is pure consciousness. You can neither see nor hear nor touch Shiva, for Shiva is beyond space and time, beyond the known universe. The 'old man' sitting before him, visible and tangible to his senses, was just a shell, a form created at will, there was nothing or none inside the shell. Like a reflection—it looks real, but there's no substance there, nothing inside. *Hiding in plain sight*. He understood at that moment what was really happening. *Yoga Maya*.

The Return

It was late evening by the time Adi got back to the Phurkia rest house. Ira and her friends were waiting for him, and the caretaker was setting up the bonfire for the night. Ira hugged Adi as he walked in.

'Did you visit the temple?' She asked. 'And did you get to meet the Babaji?'

He smiled at her. 'The temple is in ruins, no one goes there.'

Adi didn't say anything about the Babaji.

'You missed the glacier though,' Monica said, giving Adi a friendly hug. 'It was lovely!'

'Hey,' John said, waving to Adi. 'Welcome back! Ready for a drink?'

Adi smiled at John. 'Always ready!'

'I'll get the drinks!' John said. 'Deva can get the bonfire going.'

By the time the fire was lit and they had poured themselves their drinks, the sun had set and the first stars were visible against the gathering darkness of the sky.

'Cheers!' Deva said, raising his glass. 'Let's drink to the stars!'

'Cheers!' Everyone chorused, raising their glasses together.

'So, tell us about your solo trek,' Monica said. 'Did you go to the temple, and did you meet your Babaji?'

Adi lit a cigar, taking his time to respond. What was there to tell, anyway? In a real-world sense, nothing really happened—he went into an abandoned house, rested for a couple of hours, and came back. 'I found an old, abandoned house, apparently no one's lived there for years,' he said slowly. 'I waited in that house for more than an hour for Babaji to show up, but he didn't.'

'You waited in an abandoned house?' Monica asked.

'There was a patio behind the house, and an old chair. I sat on it to rest my feet for a while but dozed off. When I woke up, it was late afternoon, so I rushed back to reach here before dark.'

'And here we were,' Monica said with clear disappointment in her voice, 'thinking that you were in some stimulating dialogue with a hundred-year-old yogi in his ashram!'

Adi shrugged and took a swig of the rum. He caught the caretaker looking rather intently at him. 'So, there was no Babaji!' Adi said, turning to the caretaker.

The caretaker shrugged too. 'I didn't expect you to meet Babaji, Sir. No one has seen him for years!'

'Which means there *is* no Babaji!' John said firmly. 'A village legend!'

'The mountains are full of such legends!' Deva said solemnly. 'Legends of old yogis, ghosts, haunted houses, and all that!'

'But a real Babaji would have been interesting!' Ira said wistfully, resting her palm on Adi's knee. 'But you got to see the temple at least!'

Adi nodded. 'That I did!'

'Cheers to that then,' John said, raising his glass in the air.

'And to the Babaji who was not!' Monica joined in.

'Who owns that old house?' Adi asked, turning to the caretaker. 'And how old is it?'

'That house was built by the British, and it would be nearly a hundred years old for sure.'

'So, it is not Babaji's house, is it?'

'No, but it is said that Babaji would use it whenever he needed to. Of course, that was long ago too.'

'I see,' said Adi nodding to the caretaker. 'Well, thank you!'

The caretaker walked back to the guest house, wondering when Babaji would make his appearance. Long ago, his grandfather had told him that Babaji meets only those whom he chooses to meet. He himself had gone up several times to the old house but had not met anyone ever. And he never found any sign of anyone using that house either. Yet, deep inside him, he had not lost hope that he would meet Babaji someday. *Life is long…*

≈

Later that night, the caretaker came up to Adi while he was sitting alone on the boulder behind the rest house, smoking.

'Excuse me, Sir,' the caretaker said, clearing his throat. 'Sorry to intrude.'

'No, no, not a problem,' Adi said gently. 'Is there something you want?'

'Yes, Sir,' the caretaker said. 'If you can spare a few minutes.'

'Of course, go ahead.'

'My grandfather once told me that Babaji is real but not everyone can meet him. Only those chosen by him can see him or get to meet him.'

'Do you know of anyone who has actually met Babaji?' Adi asked.

The caretaker shook his head. 'No, Sir, no one that I know of.'

'Your grandfather? Did he know of anyone meeting Babaji?'

'No, Sir,' the caretaker said, shaking his head again.

Adi looked straight at the caretaker. 'Even if someone did actually meet Babaji, someone that Babaji chose to meet, do you think they would come down and share that openly?'

The caretaker thought for a while. 'No, Sir,' he finally said. 'Highly unlikely!'

Adi nodded silently.

The caretaker stood quietly for a few moments and then turned to go.

'Is your grandfather alive?' Adi asked as the caretaker turned.

'No, Sir,' the caretaker replied. 'He died a few years ago.'

And with that, the caretaker walked away.

Adi closed his eyes, feeling the cold night air on his skin. He had only a light jacket on. He was wholly aware of the sensation of cold but there was no thought of cold in his head, no shivering of the body. *Consciousness does not feel heat or cold…*

≈

Ira was reading a book, tucked into her sleeping bag, when he stepped back into the room.

'Hey,' Adi smiled at her, 'You still awake?'

'Don't have to wake up early,' she smiled back. 'Aren't you cold?'

'I was just contemplating that.' Adi replied.

'Contemplating whether you're feeling cold or not?'

'Well, you see,' replied Adi, stroking his chin thoughtfully. 'It is only the body that feels the cold.'

'Ah, profound insight!' Ira chuckled. 'But tell me, did you go up to the temple?'

'No, Ira, I didn't. Not physically, at least.'

'Not physically? How else could you have gone?'

'I was taken into the temple in my subtle body, while my physical body slept in the patio of the old house.'

She sat up, staring at him. She couldn't understand a single word. 'Are you high?'

Adi smiled. 'No, perfectly sober.'

'And are you serious?'

'Yes, I am!'

'You were taken into the temple?'

'Yes.'

'By whom?'

'Babaji.'

'Oh! Then you did meet him?'

'He manifested himself to me.'

'What does that mean, manifested himself?'

'Yogis can do that, it's a siddhi. They can make themselves appear, in the body, anywhere, anytime they choose. Even if they are not actually there!'

'Oh! And why did he not just meet you, like normal people?'

'Because he was not actually there. You see, he doesn't live in the physical body anymore.'

Ira stared, nonplussed.

'Let me explain. Yogis can attain faculties and powers through their sadhana that would seem impossible to us. Babaji was a very advanced yogi, a *mahayogi*. He lived four hundred years ago and was the head priest of that temple I saw in my dream.'

'Wait, did you just say he lived four hundred years ago?' Ira asked incredulously.

'Yes, more or less.'

'So, he is dead,' Ira continued, 'for all practical purposes, right?'

'No, not really. Mahayogis don't die. They can drop their physical bodies at will and continue to live in their subtle bodies, in non-physical dimensions, and can manifest themselves in the physical plane whenever they choose to. You see, they move across planes and dimensions of existence just as easily as we move from one physical location to another.'

Ira was now sitting up straight on the bed, hardly breathing.

'They play around with space and time as we play around with matter and energy.' Adi completed, apparently relieved that he could share everything without seriously challenging Ira's sanity.

There was a long, pregnant pause broken only by the sound of the rustling leaves outside.

'So, he gave you the dreams of the temple? And brought you to this place?' she said finally.

Adi nodded.

'But why?' she asked after a while. 'Why all this?'

'I was his pupil, his apprentice at the temple, four hundred years ago.' Adi replied.

Ira got out of her sleeping bag. 'I need to clear my head,' she said. 'Can we go sit outside near the fire. It would still be smouldering, I'm sure.'

'Good idea,' said Adi as he led Ira out of the room.

They returned to the bonfire, its embers still smouldering, and pulled their chairs close, just beyond the reach of the drifting smoke.

'You were with Babaji, as his apprentice, four hundred years ago?' Ira asked once they had settled.

'Yes, Ira,' Adi replied. 'And he took me to the temple, just as it was four hundred years ago. I sat there with him, in the inner chamber of the temple, meditating in his presence.'

The sounds of the smouldering fire and rustling leaves filled the air.

'And he gave me his yoga.' Adi added after a pause.

'He taught you his yoga while you were with him in the temple?'

'He did not teach or lecture me; he joined his consciousness with mine and the yoga flowed from his consciousness into mine—it came through inner dialogues, ideas and images, dreams, experiences. Difficult to explain, really. Outwardly, it was all quite normal—we were eating food, drinking tea, going for walks, sitting near a fireplace, just as we would do if he were physically present, and yet, everything was happening in a different dimension, a different order of reality. You won't understand unless you experience something like this for yourself!'

'And then you woke up, on that chair in the patio?'

'Yes, when I woke up, I realized that a few hours had passed, and it was late afternoon. I rushed back because I wanted to reach here before dark.'

'Did you check the old house again, on your way out?'

'I did. There was no sign at all of anyone having used that place in many years. There was no sign of fire, no mats or blankets, nothing, in fact!'

'So, you could've dreamed it all?' Ira suggested gently. A dream seemed more likely, and more acceptable, to Ira at that moment.

'No, it was a totally waking experience,' Adi said. 'But then, waking, dreaming and sleeping are all relative states—one person's wakefulness may be another's sleep and dream!'

Ira let it all sink in. *If not a dream, then what?*

'The important thing,' Adi said, 'is to understand the yoga.'

'But that will take time, won't it?'

'Well, the yoga is not a body of knowledge to be understood but the seeding of a new consciousness that will unfold on its own as my own inner states stabilize. This much is clear.'

'That's interesting! Babaji planted the seed of a new consciousness in you through his yoga?'

'The yoga has opened in me the possibility of a new consciousness.'

'I always thought yoga was a system or a practice, or what you just called a body of knowledge.'

'Depends on the yoga.'

'Is it a bit like the yoga given by Krishna to Arjun?'

'Yes, that is a good comparison. What Krishna gave to Arjun was also the seed of a new consciousness.'

'And it was directly transferred to Arjun's consciousness, not taught to him.' Ira added. 'I'm wondering if I can get it from you the way you received it from Babaji? Not right now of course, but whenever I'm ready for it!'

'That is not in my hands, Ira. The yoga will come from Shiva, and Shiva will decide how to give it to you.'

Ira frowned. 'So, I will have to wait?'

'Wait and invoke.'

'Invoke?'

'Invoke Shiva. Know that he resides in your heart and then invoke him in your heart with all your faith, your *shraddha*.'

'Is there a mantra to invoke Shiva?'

'Any mantra that comes to you.'

'Om namah shivaya?'

'That is a powerful mantra.'

'What does it exactly mean?'

'Om is the seed invocation, the *moola mantra*. *Namah* invokes the shraddha, the obeisance, the surrender. And Shiva is the absolute being and consciousness. This mantra is also known to the yogis as the *panchakshar* or the five-syllabled mantra, and the syllables represent and invoke the five fundamental elements of the universe—earth, water, fire, air and space.'

Ira closed her eyes, concentrating on Adi's words.

'May Shiva's grace enter Ira's heart and awaken her to her highest truth.' Adi invoked Shiva in his heart. 'Om namah shivaya!'

≈

And that night, as Ira went to sleep invoking Shiva, Adi went back to the boulder alone. He lit himself a cigar, and lay down on the boulder, staring up into the night sky. His consciousness rose into the sky with his gaze, higher and higher, till it dissolved among the stars. And then, the great silence came upon him.

Everything suddenly became utterly still. His head, in an instant, became empty and he felt his very brain become immobile. An invisible wave of silence swept away the world from his senses. The rest house, the stones and boulders, the trees, the hills and mountain peaks in the distance, everything faded away. Like a running movie fading off the screen.

No feeling, no reaction arose in him—no trepidation, no curiosity, no question, no urge to know what was happening. A massive wave of solid peace engulfed him, rendering him completely passive, almost unconscious. Except that he was not unconscious at all, he had never been so totally conscious, so completely awake before, and it was an intense wakefulness, almost like staring into the sun.

But none of all this moved him at that time. There was perhaps no 'him' left anymore to think, feel or reflect. What he had always known or experienced as himself was no longer recognizable or experienceable as a self at all—he had become a sea of consciousness, spreading everywhere, penetrating everything, vast and impersonal. There was no trace left of person or personality, just an overwhelming sense of being.

And then slowly, in some little corner of his being, he became aware of the old temple that he had experienced in another time and dimension. He became aware of the inner chamber of the temple, of the dense quietude, of the deep glow of white light emanating from the fathomless depths of the Shivalinga in the centre of the temple. And then the Shivalinga dissolved into his awareness and only the awareness remained, vast, luminous and timeless, an awareness intensely aware of itself.

When the normal mental consciousness came back to Adi, the dark of the night was passing into the first faint glow of the dawn. The sky was still lit up with stars, but the brightness of the stars was diminishing in the growing light of the dawn. His cigar had fallen to the ground and gone out long ago. He stood up quietly and brushed off the dust from the seat of his pants. He stretched his arms and legs and felt the blood rush through them. There was no thought, no movement of mind.

Somewhere in the distance, a dog was barking. With the great silence now inside of him—in his head, his brain, his limbs, perhaps even in the cells of his body—he walked back slowly into the rest house. He walked very deliberately, as if getting used to the gravity of a new planet. Everything around him, even his own body, felt somewhat hollow and unreal, as if he was witnessing it all from outside of himself—he was no longer in the body, the body now seemed to be in him. It was a strange feeling. When he entered his room, he saw Ira still fast asleep on the bed, in a world that had somehow detached from him, floating soundlessly in his consciousness, no longer enveloping him. He sat down noiselessly on the bed, beside Ira's sleeping body, barely breathing.

He knew, at that moment, that he would never be the same person again. In fact, he would never be a *person* again. He made no attempt whatsoever to understand—nothing needs to be understood or explained, only lived as quietly as possible.

Threshold

By the time they were back in Saung, Adi's mind was firmly established in the brahmic silence—no thought entered his mind, no emotion arose to disturb the tranquillity of his being. The sense of time and personal significance had faded entirely from his mind and heart, and all in him was now identified with the witness consciousness he had become, vast, impersonal, no longer limited to a body or mind, but expanding into all existences, into all forms, as if everyone everywhere was his own projection. What he had once known as ego, in himself and in others, now seemed a completely artificial and childish mechanism. All life and being, he now knew intimately, were expressions of one single living reality beyond name and description.

They reached the guest house late in the afternoon. The caretakers greeted them as they stepped in. The dog came up barking excitedly. 'We do hope that you enjoyed your trek,' the elder caretaker said, 'your rooms are ready, and the water is heated. We will set up the wood for the bonfire.'

'Superb!' Deva remarked. 'Looking forward to that.'

They had drinks and dinner around the bonfire and John, Deva and Monica retired early to their rooms. Adi decided to stay a while longer to smoke a cigar.

'Can I sit with you?' Ira asked Adi. 'I promise I won't talk.'

Adi smiled, lighting his cigar. 'Of course. Let's watch the flames together.'

So, they sat quietly with each other and watched the crackling flames while Adi smoked.

Everything was inside Adi. The fire, the forest and the hills, the breeze and the sky, Ira's mind and body, everything was within his consciousness, there was no outside. The world itself was an extension of his own being. But, in his mind, Adi knew that there was no such thing as his own being, being was universal, boundless, fathomless. He himself, like Ira, was a formation and extension of an infinite being.

He felt a slight movement in his mind and immediately became attentive.

It was Ira. She was probing him with her eyes, gently, lovingly. He could sense her affection, her attraction, her possessiveness, ripple across his being. He sensed the waves rising in her mind—she wanted desperately to talk, there were questions raging in her. And he also knew that she did not wish to disturb him.

Adi turned to Ira and smiled at her. 'We can talk; you won't be disturbing me.'

She smiled back. 'You can read my mind now?'

'Yes, you have become completely transparent to me.'

'What do you mean by transparent?'

'Your thoughts, feelings, intentions, memories are all transparent to me.'

'But you've known me better than anyone else.'

'We know each other only through our mental filters and past conditionings, Ira. Now, there are no filters. I know you exactly as you are and are meant to be, no veils or masks at all.'

'And this is how it is with everyone else too? Even the caretakers?'

'Yes.'

'Wow! That's amazing. A superpower!'

'Not really,' Adi said. 'This is how it was always meant to be amongst humans.'

'How?' Ira asked. 'Complete transparency? No veils or masks?'

'Yes, absolutely. Why would we need veils and masks?'

'But it's not practical or prudent to be utterly transparent to others. Almost like being naked.'

'What's wrong with that?'

'What about privacy? What about personal matters, personal lives?'

'How do you feel with me right now,' Adi asked, 'now that you know I can read you like an open book?'

Ira thought for a moment. 'Very self-conscious, knowing that nothing is hidden from you.'

'So, will that change anything between us?' Adi asked.

'Our relationship *will* change—I can see that. The way we communicate will change. Imagine living with someone who can see through you all the time. No secrets, no surprises, no hidden agenda!'

'And will that not be a good thing? For our relationship?'

Ira nodded. 'Yes, but for it to be ideal, it must be both ways. I should be able to see through you as well.'

'So, imagine a world where all humans become transparent to each other, and within themselves. No veils or masks, no hidden agendas, no deception, pretence, hypocrisy, or lies.'

'That would be utopian!'

'Absolutely! And every utopia must be replaced by a still higher and more beautiful utopia.'

'Will there be a perfect utopia, a utopia of utopias?'

'That will be perfect existence, perfect consciousness.'

'And is there such a thing? Perfect existence and consciousness?'

'At the end of the rainbow of our being and becoming!'

'You're no longer sounding like a philosopher,' Ira said with a chuckle. 'You're sounding religious, like a prophet!'

'Who knows?' Adi shrugged. 'Maybe I *am* becoming religious!'

Ira said nothing to that. The fire was beginning to burn out and the breeze was picking up.

'Shall we go in?' Adi asked. 'You must be tired?'

Ira stood up. 'Tired? No way. I still have so many questions.'

She put her hand in Adi's and said, 'Let's go for a walk while I pester you with my questions!'

Holding hands, Adi and Ira walked away from the bonfire.

'Will there be place for human love at the end of the rainbow, Adi?' she asked him as they walked out into the forest.

'Ah, there's no way of knowing that. By then, human beings would have changed from what they are now. The present human form will not be able to contain a higher consciousness, leave alone a perfect one.'

'The human form itself will change with the change in consciousness?'

'For sure. I was given that experience. Babaji gave up the physical form not because he wished to avoid physical dissolution but because he realized that the consciousness he had attained could not be contained in the ordinary human form. The ordinary human form is severely limited, as is the ordinary human mind.'

'What is Babaji's present form like? Is it still human?'

'He can assume any form he wants to—man or woman, human or *daivic*, flesh or spirit. It doesn't matter.'

'So, that wouldn't be human at all, would it?'

'It is a future human form, Ira. As humans evolve in consciousness, they will outgrow the limited physical body and mind. This sack of flesh we call the body will be discarded like rag, or changed to something else entirely.'

'And the mind too?'

'The mind will expand into cosmic consciousness, no longer tethered to an individual brain and nervous system.'

'And Babaji is all this?'

'Yes, he is all this. And perhaps more, who knows?'

'Can you meet him again?'

'I don't need to.'

'I don't understand.'

'He has revealed the inmost self to me, the atman, the pure consciousness. Once you know that, you know all things and beings intimately, as your own self. You or Babaji, there is no difference.'

'There is no difference between me and Babaji?' Ira asked incredulously.

'There is no difference anywhere. Like millions of waves rising out of the sea and falling back into it. Think about it, Ira—once you know the sea, will any of the waves matter?'

'And your inmost self is the sea?'

'Precisely. Knowing which, all is known.'

'So, I am a wave rising in your being?'

'We are all waves of self-becoming rising in pure being. We—you and I, and everyone else, from the caretakers to Babaji—are waves of self-becoming, and self is atman, pure being. Are you getting it now?'

'So, we are the becomings of the atman?'

'Yes. We are all formations of atman. We exist as waves at one level, and as sea at another. It's all one substance, one movement. When we realize ourselves as sea, we do not cease to be waves, but then, we become conscious waves of the sea, conscious of our source and reality. That is enlightenment, that is liberation. The wave is liberated into the sea without ceasing to be wave.'

They walked slowly, still hand in hand, for a long time. The night was getting colder and breezier.

'Now I understand—this universe is the self-becoming of one single being!' Ira said almost in a whisper. 'That is how we are all one. That is how you know me from within, that is how I am transparent to you.'

'Yes, Ira,' Adi replied. 'You're getting it!'

'And this being is Shiva? Shiva is absolute consciousness?'

'Doesn't matter what one calls it—when you realize the inmost self, names and descriptions become irrelevant.'

'And I am that inmost self, the atman?'

'That is the source, the origin.'

'And when I realize that source, the I will dissolve in it?'

'Yes.'

'Then who will realize?'

Adi turned to Ira and smiled. 'You're getting close!'

'What do you mean by that?'

'The ripeness for the yoga…'

'Are *you* doing something?'

'I am merely a *nimitta*, an instrument. Just as Babaji was.'

'But just by being with you, things will happen, right?'

'I believe so.'

'You're being modest, Adi.'

'No, I'm being honest. I have no idea what will happen to anyone because of me, or through me. It is Shiva's presence that works through me. What happens to you, or anyone else, is Shiva's will, not mine. I can only invoke him for you. Shall we turn back? It's getting late.'

'So, does time exist?' Ira asked.

Adi chuckled. 'You're picking up fast, my dear. Time may not exist in a real sense but the bus for Almora *will* leave at 10 am tomorrow, and there *will* be a tomorrow.'

'And what will happen if we don't take the bus at 10 tomorrow?'

'In what dimension of being?'

'In the only one that matters to me and you.'

'Well, then, nothing will happen. There will be many more buses and many more tomorrows.'

'So, why don't we keep walking?'

'Why not, as the philosopher in me would ask.'

'Is there still a philosopher in you, Adi?'

'I don't know. Maybe there's more of the prophet than the philosopher now!' Adi laughed.

Ira and Adi turned around and started walking back to the rest house.

'So, Adi, nothing and no one is outside of us, right? There is no outside at all. Everything is within.'

'Yes, an infinite within of being.'

'Then, there's none to know this within as there is none outside to know?'

'Thus,' Adi said quietly, 'the atman is unknowable.'

'What then is the point of it all?'

'Don't look for any point. Just look at the thing, look at what is.'

'It is dawning on me that since atman is unknowable, we are all, in essence, unknowable.'

'Not just we, everything is unknowable.'

'Knowledge is an illusion?'

'Till the Self is known, all is illusion and ignorance. This is what our great seers used to say.'

'And Self cannot be known, as you have just established.'

'Knowledge by identity, Ira, knowledge by becoming what you seek to know.'

'And that is the yoga?'

'That seems to be the threshold of the yoga.'

The First Crossing

36 Days after the Trek

Adi closed his eyes and plunged into the depths of his being, like plunging into the dark depths of a sea. He withdrew his mind layer by layer from the manifest universe till he could feel nothing, not even his own consciousness. Space and time dissolved in that plunge, and the universe itself unravelled, returning in timeless swiftness, to its mystical origin that no embodied consciousness would ever know. And there, in that fathomless, inscrutable depth of being, he knew himself for the first time—not an individuality, nor even a cosmos, but that which was plunging infinitely into itself, every atom of existence exploding into tidal waves of pure bliss. All that he had ever known and become dissolved in that unspeakable bliss. And then, all that remained of him was a dimensionless luminosity.

His being hovered upon the threshold of the manifest universe, the very edge of time, where all could turn to existence, or to void, in the blink of an eye. There, at that precipitous edge of an impenetrable void, he touched the presence that was at once his own source and the source of all being—a presence out of which universes rose and fell in an instant, a presence that was everything and everyone simultaneously, in a single incomprehensible movement of being and becoming. In that single movement, there was no beginning or end, no time, no division—everything was and is, simultaneously and seamlessly. Universes upon universes, like infinitesimal fluctuations of that presence, appeared and disappeared in blissful, dancing waves of light.

≈

When he finally returned to mind and form, it was dark and quiet around him. He could only hear some distant, unfamiliar sounds. Adi had no recollection of where he was, but that didn't matter—place and time were of little consequence to him. He couldn't feel his body, there was just a sense of bare physical existence, without dimension or weight. He closed his eyes and waited, barely breathing. When he opened his eyes, dawn was just beginning to break across the eastern sky.

≈

Ira entered the room quietly. He did not see her but felt her presence, her movement. He opened his eyes, and as he did so, his familiar universe came flooding back to his mind and senses. He knew perfectly well that this universe was a formation of his own consciousness, and so was Ira. He also knew that he himself was a formation in Ira's consciousness. *Maze of infinite mirrors…*

'You've been in dhyana for two days now!' she said softly, not wanting to disturb him. 'Shall I open the window? It's morning.'

Adi nodded, and Ira opened the large window opening out to the woods behind their house. The early morning sunlight streamed in, lighting up the meditation room.

'Two days?' Adi repeated slowly, finding his voice again. It seemed to Ira that Adi was speaking from some great distance. But Ira was now getting used to Adi's frequent and prolonged withdrawals from waking consciousness. More than a month had passed since their return from the Pindari trek and Adi's mystical encounter with Babaji. Since their return, Ira had plunged into the study of the Upanishads to better appreciate Adi's inner journey. Under Adi's guidance, she had progressed much in her meditations. She also knew that she was drawing psychic energy directly from Adi, which was helping her open to the yoga rapidly. It was a rare privilege to be in a personal relationship with a realized being. Like the consorts of the rishis of old!

'I didn't quite realize that. Have I missed anything?' Adi asked, looking innocently at Ira.

She smiled at Adi. 'You know that you wouldn't miss anything here. Everything that can happen has already happened in Shiva's eternal consciousness.'

'Well, it is not as straight as that,' Adi said slowly. 'It's more of a play of possibilities, infinite possibilities playing across multiple planes and dimensions. And Shiva does not determine the outcome of this play. The outcome is determined at one level by the gunas and the forces of prakriti, at another level, by the infinite variations human beings bring into the play.'

'Human beings can influence the outcome of a cosmic play?'

'Of course. Human beings are part of the play, aren't they? Human intentions, desires, fears, our actions and reactions, everything we are and do, subtly or not so subtly, are continuously affecting the play of the possibilities, across all planes.'

'So, what about divine intervention?'

'The Divine will not intervene, unless there is a strong possibility of a catastrophic collapse.'

'The *dharma yuddha* of the Mahabharata?'

'Yes, and the dawning of the *kaliyug*.'

'But such interventions are rare, I understand that. I'm thinking of mundane, everyday things. Like wars, riots, diseases, poverty.'

'Are these catastrophic in any way?'

'Catastrophic? Perhaps not.'

'They will all pass.'

'A third world war?'

'Still not catastrophic.'

'The third world war will be nuclear, you know that, don't you?'

'Yes, I do. But when I say catastrophic, I mean in terms of evolution on earth.'

'But won't a nuclear war wipe out the human species? At least, most of it?'

'But evolution does not depend on one species, however advanced that species may be. How many mass extinctions have happened so far?'

'Five.'

'And do you know how many species have disappeared from earth since the beginning?'

Ira shook her head.

'Over 99% of all species that have ever lived on Earth are now extinct,' Adi said.

'Oh! So, what you're saying is that the human species is dispensable to evolution of consciousness?'

'Yes. Because there is a possibility of a new species emerging from the human that will take the evolution forward, to the next level.'

'So, we don't need to be worried?' Ira smiled.

'I never was!' Adi smiled back.

≈

'When you go into your dhyana for hours on end, where do you go?' Ira asked Adi that evening.

'Wherever Shiva takes me,' Adi replied. 'Higher, or deeper.'

'Higher or deeper into consciousness?'

'Yes, into consciousness. But consciousness is not like space, so higher or deeper does not mean dimensions like they do in space.'

'So, what does it mean when you say higher or deeper?'

'Relative to the human plane, and the present human consciousness.'

'You are in a higher consciousness relative to Monica, for instance.'

'And you're in a much higher consciousness relative to me?'

'Yes.'

'And Babaji?'

'Babaji was identified with Shiva.'

'And Shiva is?'

'Absolute consciousness.'

'Which is not relative to anyone?'

'That is why it is absolute. The absolute consciousness is everywhere, in everyone, in everything. There is no higher or lower, deeper or superficial, in the absolute sense.'

'But Babaji *would* be in a higher and deeper consciousness than all of us, right?'

'No, Babaji is all-consciousness, one with brahman, one with Shiva. So, he is the cosmic consciousness, at once the highest and the lowest, the deepest and the most superficial, everything.'

'But you say we are all one consciousness, so are we not all the same as Babaji?'

'It all depends on realization and identification, Ira.'

'I have to realize Shiva first?'

'Yes, realization is the first siddhi. Then the identification of mind, body and spirit.'

'Can you help me realize Shiva? I am chanting the mahamantra you gave, but it is a slow process.'

'Neither slow nor fast, Ira—it is not something that happens in time. It all depends on how much you intensify your sadhana.'

'That is where I need your help.'

Adi was quiet for a long time, as if meditating on Ira. Ira kept quiet too.

Finally, Adi said, 'You are at the threshold of the yoga, Ira. You need to cross the threshold.'

'What is that threshold that I have to cross?'

'The threshold of mental knowledge and understanding. It has brought you so far, but it can take you no farther.'

Ira let that sink in.

'What is the next step? How do I cross the threshold?'

'Still the waves of your mind.'

Waves of the mind? 'Thoughts, you mean?'

'All movements and activities of mind and intellect.'

'Whoa, that seems a tall order!'

'Yet it is the only thing you need to do in order to cross over from mind to consciousness.'

'Is there a difference between mind and consciousness?'

'The difference between a wave and the sea. When mind is free of all movements—or *chitta vritti* as the yogis call it—then it becomes pure dhyana. That dhyana itself is consciousness. In that dhyana, mind dissolves into pure consciousness, namarupa dissolves into Shiva's silence.'

'And all that remains is Shiva,' Ira whispered to herself.

'Take one step at a time, one day at a time. No haste, no push. If you truly want it, it will come to you. Like learning to play the piano, I suppose—you keep playing with the notes till you suddenly get the music.'

Mind without movement. Is that possible at all? But one must take the leap.

The Second Crossing

90 Days after the Trek

Adi and Ira sat together in the garden, sipping hot tea and enjoying the cool evening breeze. The sun was about to set, and the sky glowed a deep orange.

'I have been wondering, Adi,' Ira said, taking a sip of the tea. 'How does one do all this dhyana and stilling of the mind, and still function normally in the world?'

'One develops the knack, I suppose.' Adi said.

'Like learning to play the piano—you just get the music?'

'Yes, if you keep trying sincerely.'

'Or one becomes a sannyasi?'

'A sannyasi?' Adi repeated. 'Who's a sannyasi?'

'One who renounces the world, home and family and all that?'

'A real sannyasi renounces only ahankara and moha.'

'So, Babaji did not renounce the world, did he?'

'He did not need to. He was a self-realized being. He *was* the world.'

'But before his self-realization?'

'Who knows when he attained self-realization, or what he was before that? He did not say anything about his life or sadhana.'

'But doesn't a yogi need to renounce the world—family, relationships, ambition, money, sex and a hundred other things of this world?'

'He needs to renounce only his ahankara, his moha and maya.'

'That seems difficult!'

'It is far easier to renounce the world than to renounce one's ego and attachments.'

'So, what is the most effective way to give up the ego and attachments?'

'Realize the atman.'

'And till then? While one is trying to realize?'

'Keep the focus on the process, on the sadhana, don't get distracted by anything at all. If you focus only on Self and the process of realizing it, the other things will become irrelevant.'

Ira poured herself and Adi another cup of tea. 'There's some cake in the kitchen. Shall I get it?'

Adi nodded, sipping at the hot tea. Ira soon returned with the cakes.

Adi took a bite of the cake. 'This is good!'

'So, you can still appreciate my cake?' Ira asked, smiling back.

'And why not?' Adi asked. 'In fact, I've never enjoyed your cakes so much!'

'Seriously? The yoga has not taken away your taste buds?'

'Thankfully, it hasn't!'

'So, it does not conflict with worldly experiences?'

'Of course not. Yoga is not the struggle of the ascetic. True asceticism is quite an evolved thing!'

'What is the true asceticism? I would love to know that.'

'Total focus on the atman is asceticism. All the world's pleasures, all kinds of experiences, may wash over you, wave after wave, but you remain fixed in your concentration on the atman, fixed and firm in your devotion to it—that is the true tapasya.'

'That is indeed beautiful!' Ira said in a hushed voice. 'I always thought of tapasya as a negation of life.'

'When Krishna tells Arjuna *atma sanstham manah kritva na kinchid api chintayet*, he is talking of perhaps the highest form of tapasya—to think nothing, your whole consciousness fixed on the Self.'

Ira kept sitting with the empty cup in her hand, watching the last rays of the sun dissolve into the darkness.

≈

Ira was fast asleep. Adi came up quietly and stood beside her bed. She looked so innocent while asleep, like a baby. As he watched Ira's sleeping body on the bed, his breathing slowed. He closed his eyes and entered her consciousness, penetrating deep into the recesses of her being, filling her with luminous waves of silence and peace.

Deep in sleep, Ira saw a beam of white light descend into her heart and spread all through her body. Even in sleep, she felt the luminous contact and trembled lightly.

≈

Adi was watering the plants in the garden when he felt a vast and dense stillness descend upon him. Even the background ripples of thought in his mind died down, and there was absolute silence. A last sense of individuality—buried deep in the subconscious—dissolved into that stillness, and Adi, even as pure I-sense, died down, replaced by an all-seeing consciousness in which the world itself, with all its forms, movements and sounds, seemed to be floating like a dream object. Adi stood still, not attempting to interpret or understand. In fact, there was nothing in that all-seeing consciousness that could have been interpreted or understood. Everything was—without interpretation or explanation, without before or after, a world without narrative.

Ira stepped into the garden and looked at Adi, standing still and staring into space. She at once knew that he was in one of his trance-like states, a kind of samadhi, perhaps. She turned to go, not wanting to disturb him, when she heard his voice, clear and firm, in what seemed to be her own mind.

'No, stay.'

Ira turned and faced him. 'Sure!' she said softly. 'Want me to do the watering?'

'Yes, why not?' Again, she heard the words distinctly in her mind, inside her head.

Ira took the watering can from Adi and continued watering the plants. Adi watched. Except that there was no Adi behind the eyes. There was no Adi in the brain. The brain and the senses were simply extensions of a cosmic consciousness. Ira's form seemed empty, hollow, but not isolated—Ira's presence seemed to flow seamlessly into the plants and the flowers, and beyond the garden, outward, into space. There was no Ira, only a presence formed out of the cosmic consciousness that Adi had become. Everything, indeed, was the same presence in different formations and movements.

A bird flies across the sky. For the briefest of a moment, there is a subtle ripple in the consciousness. And then, there is no bird, no wake. The sky, as it always was, before the bird, after the bird. Indescribable. Anirvachaniya. The presence that was Ira was flowing into the presence that was Adi. Adi was Ira as Ira was Adi. There never was a difference. The differences of form and personality had dissolved in the flowing. What remained was beyond the scope of human thought or expression.

≈

Adi remained outwardly active, while inwardly absorbed in the unfolding experience of what the Vedanta calls *brahman*, the vast impersonal all-knowing and all-seeing consciousness that bears this universe, as an ocean bears its waves upon its depths. While thus absorbed, he remained mostly in his room, stepping out occasionally into the garden for a stroll by himself. Occasionally, Ira would make him tea which he would always accept with a distant smile. He hardly spoke while in that state of absorption, except for a few practical exchanges with Ira. Ira instinctively felt that Adi was in some deep yogic state and took great care not to intrude upon him. She could herself feel an atmosphere of concentrated calm around him, and would often sit quietly near him, trying to soak in that atmosphere.

After almost a week, Adi finally seemed to return to his normal self. Ira could now sense Adi's shifting moods with increasing accuracy, though he himself never expressed any of his moods or needs. Ira could feel Adi turning increasingly reticent by the day.

'Would you like to come for a walk with me?' she asked Adi, seizing an opportune moment. Adi agreed instantly. The weather was cool and crisp. And it was more than a week since Adi had stepped out of the house.

'You've been very quiet lately,' Ira said to Adi as they walked out towards the woods.

'In fact, so have you,' Adi remarked with a smile.

'That's because I don't want to disturb you when you're in one of your withdrawn moods!'

'I can sense a growing quietude in you too, Ira, and it's not all to do with my moods!' Adi remarked, still smiling.

Ira looked meaningfully at Adi. 'Something that you are doing, Adi?'

'Not what I am doing, Ira, but rather, what I am becoming.'

'Can you talk about it?' Ira asked.

'But it will not be of any relevance to you, Ira,' Adi replied. 'What I seem to be becoming wouldn't be of relevance to anyone besides myself.'

'But what is it that you seem to be becoming?'

'I can't say for sure. It's all so fluid, so undefined.'

'Some yogic experience?'

'Experience? Maybe that's not quite the word. Seems more like realizing something that has always been there.'

'Like?'

Adi's mind was thoughtless. He could understand Ira's question, even feel the wonderment, tinged with a little human concern, behind the question, but could draw no word or description out of his memory to respond to her question. There was the word *brahman* in the background of his mind, just the word, without sense or implication. Adi knew the word but there was no meaning in the word.

All meaning was lost to his mind. The buddhi seemed empty, hollow.

'What is it that you are realizing, Adi?' Ira asked again, but her words simply bounced off Adi's brain. Adi's brain was extraordinarily still, and there was a profound sense of lightness and bliss in that stillness.

Adi abruptly stopped walking and pointed to a boulder. 'Let's sit there for a while, shall we?'

Ira nodded and they walked up to the boulder. Adi sat on it, drawing up his knees. Ira sat quietly bedside him. Adi's brain was so utterly still that he lost all sense of physical boundary and separation. The brain itself seemed to be expanding beyond his body, right into the molecules of the matter around him. The boulder, the trees, the leaves, Ira's body, even the air around him seemed one single, unbroken substance.

Ira felt a silence, almost physical in its intensity, envelop her body and senses. In a few moments, her mind became empty of thought and word. All memory of her conversation with Adi disappeared into the emptiness. Even the memory of walking with Adi in the woods disappeared without a trace.

≈

'Something happened back there,' Ira said as they entered the house later in the evening. 'I remember that we had gone out for a walk, but that's all I remember—everything else seems blanked out.'

'What else was there to remember?'

'What do you remember?'

'That we went out for a walk.'

'But why?'

'Because you wanted to.'

'But how come I don't recall anything else?'

'But why should you? There was nothing else.'

'So, why does it feel that there was something else?'

'Because you had a lot of questions for me.'

'I did, didn't I? But why can't I remember them?'

'Probably because they weren't so important.'

'But I don't remember the walk either. Where did we go? How long did we walk? Where did we turn back?'

Ira looked just a bit desperate. Adi smiled, a bit amused.

'No, you're doing something, Adi. I'm sure!'

'I am?' Adi shrugged, still amused. 'I assure you, I am not doing anything. Things are happening, that's all.'

'What's happening? Come on, Adi, I know that you know.'

'Why don't we sit for a while?' Adi suggested. 'Let's have some tea.'

Ira brightened up. 'Good idea! Let me make some tea, and then we'll talk. Outside?'

'Yes, sure.'

Adi went out into the garden and sat on one of the chairs. His brain was still quiet, keenly attentive, but totally detached from all that was happening.

When Ira came back with the tea, his eyes were closed. As soon as he felt Ira's presence, he opened his eyes and smiled at her. She laid the cups of tea on the small wooden table in front of them. He picked up the cup of steaming tea and took a sip.

'Good?' Ira asked.

'Of course,' Adi replied. 'How can tea not be good?'

'I can think of a dozen ways how tea may not be good,' Ira said, smiling.

'Is that what you want to talk about?' Adi asked humorously. 'The profound mysteries of tea making?'

'Tell me, Adi, what is happening with you?'

Adi narrowed his eyes. 'The boundaries of self are dissolving.'

'But that has been happening since you met Babaji?'

'Yes, it started with him, but it goes on. As a person, I seem to be dissolving, like a lump of salt in the sea.'

'But, as a person, you're here, aren't you? We still converse, relate…'

'What you are experiencing of me right now is not what I essentially am but what I express and project of myself to you, the personality. What I essentially am, cannot be projected or expressed.'

'That is right,' Ira said, pondering. 'I can only relate to what you project. Except in flashes when the personality drops for a moment, and I catch a glimpse of what you really are. So, the person that is dissolving is the essential you?'

'Yes, the identity, the identifications, the self-becoming, all that constitutes Adi…all that is dissolving, as if, Adi is disappearing into the vast. A drop disappearing into the ocean.'

'And is something else replacing the Adi?'

'Replacing? Perhaps that's not the word. There is an uncovering. As if the Adi I knew myself to be was just layers of covering, *adhyaropa,* that is now being removed.'

Adi did not complete his sentence. He seemed drawn somewhere within. Ira waited for a while, then asked—'And what is beneath those layers?'

The question brought Adi back to the moment. 'Self without boundary, without personal identity or memory… endless expansiveness…cannot describe…the old seers used the word *brahman*…infinite being and consciousness… all-permeating…beyond personality and impersonality, beyond duality and non-duality…'

Ira sensed Adi's struggle—a philosopher, normally superbly at ease with words, struggling with words—and understood that the deeper the realizations get, the more indescribable they become. Or, perhaps, the more irrelevant for others. Even if he could have described it most eloquently, it would have made no difference to Ira, because the description by itself would have brought her no closer to the thing described. She remembered what Adi had once said, quoting Sri Aurobindo—*silence is all, say the sages*.

Her eyes lit up and she looked directly at Adi. 'Now I understand Vedanta!'

Adi looked at Ira and saw her expression and smiled. 'What do you understand?'

'The end of knowledge and knowing, *veda* and *anta*, the end of mental descriptions and explanations, the end of mental understanding. Knowledge ends in the knower.'

'What happens to your study of the Upanishads?'

'Doesn't matter now. You are there for me, a living embodiment of Vedanta, why ever would I need to study a text?'

'That will be quite a leap, Ira!'

'But isn't it true? It's like I'm thrown into a river and I'm holding on to my jug of water.'

'Hmm, so will you now follow me instead of the Upanishads?'

'And should I not?'

Adi looked quizzically at her. 'I am not the complete guru yet; I may not have the *adhikara* to lead anyone else.'

'I'm not exactly anyone else, am I? I'm your partner!'

'That you are,' Adi said warmly. '*Sahadharmi*, they say in Sanskrit—one who shares your dharma.'

'So? Doesn't that give me the *adhikar* of the *shishya*?'

'Yes, it certainly does.'

'Initiate me then.'

Adi looked closely at Ira. 'You're serious?'

'I am,' Ira said firmly.

'There's no initiation, really. I've given you Patanjali's master formula...*yogas chittavritti nirodhah*.'

'It is not as simple as it sounds.'

'See, thoughts will come to the mind—all kinds of thoughts—but you must concentrate your mind to a point where thoughts do not leave a wake. Let the thoughts come and pass, like birds flying across the sky.'

'The mind doesn't need to be totally silent?'

'No, just concentrated, self-gathered.'

'Hmm. Is there a practice?'

'Become a witness to your own mind, to your own life—unaffected, detached, impersonal. Watch the mind as you would watch a child at play. Be patient and gentle with it. No judgement, no haste, no coercion. Slowly, the mind will quieten and gather itself. And yes, keep breathing, long and deep, as you watch.'

Like learning to play the piano, Ira thought to herself.

Karma Yoga

180 Days after the Trek

Adi was sitting alone in the garden that evening, enjoying the gentle evening breeze, when Swami Vivekananda appeared to him. Adi recognized the Swami immediately and stood up. He then bent down and touched the Swami's feet with both his hands. The Swami placed his right palm on Adi's head, and softly said, '*Om tat sat*', bestowing on him the highest spiritual benediction possible in Sanatan Dharma. As the Swami's palm touched Adi's head, an electric current shot down Adi's spine, from the top of his head to the base, the location of the *muladhara chakra*. A dense white light exploded in Adi's head and flooded everything within him. In his inner being, the chaitya purusha, Adi knew immediately that he was in the presence of Shiva himself. All he could form in the depths of his consciousness were the five syllables of the great mantra, *Om namah Shivaya*, in greeting.

Vivekananda looked deep into Adi's eyes, and smiled, a smile radiant with love and compassion. In that one look, Vivekananda compressed all that he wanted to convey to Adi. For Adi, it was a spiritual fulfilment beyond every siddhi, every realization. In complete gratitude, he closed his eyes, absorbing the divine presence.

As he closed his eyes, he saw himself seated in the inner chamber of the temple he had once lived and studied in.

Facing him was Shiva, his Guru and the temple priest. Behind Shiva was the light of pure consciousness that seemed to be illuminating the universe from within. The stars and the nebulae were no longer in outer space but whirling and dancing in Adi's inmost mind. All existence for Adi converged into a single stream of self-becoming that was Adi, and Shiva, and Vivekanand simultaneously. The being he had known to be himself dissolved into Shiva, and the being he had known to be Shiva dissolved into Vivekananda's luminous presence, and Vivekananda's presence merged into the pure light of consciousness that was glowing behind Shiva's form.

≈

Ira and Adi sat together for breakfast next morning.

As Adi took a spoonful of hot porridge, he smiled at Ira. 'Slept well?'

'Yes, there was a kind of solid peace in the air last night. Anything to do with your meditation?'

'Vivekananda came to me last evening,' Adi said.

Ira looked up from her bowl of porridge, her spoon held midair. '*Swami Vivekananda*?'

Adi nodded.

Ira smiled to herself, remembering that she was with a self-realized yogi—so, why not? She brought the spoon into her mouth. She had given up trying to mentally understand Adi's realizations and experiences. She would wait for Adi to say something on his own. Her own concentration was deepening by the day. She was now able to observe her mental activities and movements and strike down thoughts or images before they could become distractions. It wasn't always easy, but she was developing the knack. The more she observed her mind, the more she realized that most of her distractions were inconsequential and avoidable. When you realize that most of your mental 'stuff' is useless, then it all becomes easier.

They finished their porridge silently. There was no rush or impatience in any of them. Life had settled into a gentle and harmonious rhythm between the two of them.

'Vivekananda's visit has opened the being to higher possibilities,' Adi said, pouring tea into his cup. 'It will be interesting to observe what happens after this.'

'Vivekananda, they say, was an *ansha* of Shiva,' Ira said.

'Yes, though I don't know what they mean by *ansha*. Shiva is Shiva, one and indivisible. You cannot have portions of Shiva.'

'You often say that all parts are wholes.'

'Yes, a part of Shiva is the whole of Shiva, a portion of reality is the whole of reality. But tell me, how was your day?'

'Quiet,' she said. 'Not much happening. I'm reaching a stability in the dhyana. And I'm enjoying the editing too. Much more than I used to before my practice.'

'Yes, that often happens!' Adi finished his tea and kept aside the empty cup. 'Dhyana enhances the quality of everything you do.'

'Yes, the work is not only more enjoyable but, somehow, more meaningful. Everything becomes meaningful, even making tea or cooking meals.'

'That is the beginning of karma yoga, Ira. When you begin to experience the rasa of all actions.'

'We must talk of karma yoga someday, Adi.'

'Have you not read the Bhagavad Gita?'

'Yes, I have. But now I want it from you.'

'I'm hardly the karma yogi, Ira.'

'You're a jnana yogi, I know, but does that stop you from telling me about karma yoga?'

'I don't think it does,' Adi smiled, picking up an apple. 'Is there something specific about karma yoga that interests you?'

'What is perfect action, Adi?'

'When Krishna, the divine self, acts through you, using you as nimitta.'

'When does that happen?'

'When intention and action both are liberated from the sense of personal doership.'

'How is one to act in this world without ego? Is not the ego behind all our intentions and actions?'

'The ego is fabrication of the mind. Find out what really wills and acts in you.'

'The Gita tells us that it is prakriti, through her gunas, that wills and acts through us.'

'But prakriti by herself is inert, unconscious, she only reflects Krishna's consciousness, as the moon that has no light of its own only reflects the light of the sun.'

'So, it is Krishna that moves our will and action?'

'Yes, but not always directly. The divine will is filtered and distorted through several layers of subtle and gross prakriti. The pure and direct divine will can only be known and manifested through yoga with Krishna.'

'Yoga with Krishna?'

'To be always concentrated on Krishna, to live in his consciousness, identified in mind and will with him—that is the yoga with Krishna.'

'When you speak of karma, Adi, you speak of Krishna, not Shiva—is there a reason?'

'It's the same thing, Ira. Shiva and Krishna are two aspects of the same divine self, the same brahman.'

'I understand,' said Ira. 'How to engage in action when we are still *sadhaks*, ordinary people driven by ego and the play of the gunas.'

'Be vigilant, be conscious, that is all. Watch the play of the gunas, see how the figment of the ego becomes such a real thing for us. And as you watch, with a keen and focused mind, the play will become increasingly transparent to your inner vision.'

'That I am doing, more and more. I see far better now than I ever did.'

'While you do that, bring love into all your works and actions. Find the divine rasa of action in all that you do.'

'Sometimes, I find that I'm working not for the rasa but for the money.'

'There is nothing wrong with money, the problem is with *moha* and *lobha*.'

'Lobha, I understand, but what exactly is moha?'

'Identification and attachment, the root of the me-and-mine thought.'

'But isn't it because of lobha in me that I still work for money?'

'Money is a practical necessity, Ira. None can avoid that entirely.'

'You seem to have done that, Adi.'

'Oh, that's because I never needed to work for money, thanks to my family Trust.'

'But what if you didn't have your family wealth and the Trust? What would you have done to earn a livelihood?'

'That is an entirely hypothetical question, Ira. The Adi that I am in this lifetime is the outcome of the karma for this lifetime. A different line of karma would have made a different kind of Adi with several different lines of karmic possibilities.'

'Is it all karma then?'

'But what is karma?'

'The fruits of all your intentions and actions in your past lives, isn't it? At least that is what I've been told.'

'That's a rather simplistic understanding. Karma is more complex than that.'

'Can you explain?'

'Each of us, in every lifetime and every dimension, represents a certain possibility in the evolution of life and consciousness. For instance, Adi, in this lifetime, represents the possibility of self-realization. For that possibility to manifest, circumstances and events are lined up, or orchestrated, by the divine intelligence around Adi so that Adi can realize his highest possibility within this lifetime, which is self-realization. This whole mechanism is what we mean by karma.'

'Wow, not so easy to grasp,' said Ira. 'So, your family being wealthy was to create the right conditions for you to realize your possibility?'

'Yes. But then, my family being wealthy was not for my benefit alone. Many others also benefited; many were affected in many ways. For instance, our family gardener's son, who couldn't have afforded basic schooling, could go to England for his higher education and come back a highly accomplished doctor—who then went on to set up a hospital in his village that directly or indirectly benefitted the entire village. So, you see, karma works in multiple planes and dimensions, across multiple lifetimes and timelines, touching countless individuals in countless ways. It's impossible for the human mind to grasp the entirety of karma and its workings.'

'From what I'm grasping, Adi, karma is not individual but cosmic in its working. Am I right?'

'Yes, you are. Nothing is just individual, Ira, everything is cosmic. Even the individual is cosmic. Do you think my self-realization is of any use to me individually?'

'Well, isn't it?'

'No, Ira, for the simple reason that self-realization erases individuality completely, it's never of any use to any individual. Self-realization is always cosmic, and through every individual who attains to self-realization, the universe grows towards its own perfection.'

'So, through this cosmic network of karma, that somehow shapes all beings, events and circumstances, the universe grows towards its own highest possibility?'

'Yes, Ira, that is how it works.'

'And, in that case, there is no good or bad karma then. Or, at least, there is no bad karma!'

'Outside the human mind, there is no good or bad anyway!'

'Now I understand what it means when you say that everything is divine Grace.'

Adi smiled. 'And why I don't have to worry about money?'

'I think I do,' Ira said. 'At least I understand that it has nothing to do with your family wealth.'

'You see, Ira,' Adi explained, 'it has nothing to do with wealth at all, it's to do with the logic of karma that I understand and accept. The logic of karma in everyone's life is infallible, everything is perfectly arranged and orchestrated. Whatever happens, or does not happen, follows from the infallible logic of karma.'

'So, if all the wealth you have were to disappear this instant, you wouldn't fret about it?'

'No, I wouldn't,' Adi said.

'What then would be your reaction?'

'Why should there always be a reaction?'

'No, I mean what would you do?'

'Be quiet. And wait.'

'Wait for what?'

'For karma to work itself out. Remember what I just explained—all karma is cosmic, there is nothing individual. What you see as individual good fortune or misfortune, good or bad, is always a little part of a cosmic working. If you wait, the whole thing will unravel in your consciousness.'

'So, worrying and fretting would be perfectly useless from a cosmic perspective?'

'From the cosmic perspective, all individual events are momentary bubbles in spacetime.'

'So, from that perspective, for one living in cosmic consciousness, wouldn't it be possible to tweak the workings of karma a bit? To avert some misfortune, for instance?'

'But why would someone living in cosmic consciousness do that? Wouldn't he then see the whole cosmic web of causes and effects, of karmic possibilities across lifetimes and individuals, and would know exactly why things are happening the way they are—good or bad, fortunate or unfortunate, happy or unhappy—and would not change even one little jot?'

'For to change one little thing would be interfering with all cosmic karma?'

'Precisely.'

'So, maharshis and such higher beings don't interfere with cosmic events at all?'

'Only in the rarest of cases where intervention is absolutely needed.'

'Where then is the scope for divine Grace?'

'Divine Grace is everywhere, in everything, woven into the very fabric of our existence. The very cosmic web of karma is an expression of divine Grace.'

'Difficult to understand divine Grace,' Ira said with a sigh.

'Even the gods do not understand it.' Adi said with a smile.

'When we speak of divine Grace, Adi, whose grace is it—Shiva's? Krishna's?'

'Remember that Shiva and Krishna are simply two aspects of the same divine. The very presence of the Divine is grace, Ira. Wherever the Divine is, there the grace is. When we say grace is woven into the fabric of our existence, we mean the Divine itself is woven into the fabric of our existence.'

'Ah! Now it's clear. So, invoking Shiva is invoking the grace. It's the same thing.'

'Yes, it's all one. Shiva is Ishvara, Krishna is Ishvara, if we must give it a name. In deeper truth, Ishvara is the supreme self, our inmost self, atman. When one realizes atman, one realizes Ishvara, one realizes Shiva, one realizes Narayan.'

'Someday I shall realize atman…' Ira whispered wistfully.

Adi smiled. 'But you already are atman!'

Ira was quiet for a long time before she responded. 'Then how is it that I don't know it?'

'Don't know what?'

'That I am atman?'

'Who is this I that does not know?'

Ira reflected. 'The buddhi.'

'But buddhi is not conscious in itself.'

'It is by the atman that buddhi is sentient and intelligent,' Ira said, recalling the Upanishads.

'When the buddhi becomes quiet,' said Adi, 'withdrawing into its source, the atman shines through.'

'That is why the buddhi will never know the atman,' said Ira. 'One cannot know that by which all is known.'

'That, Ira, is the old jnana!'

'I understand once again why you keep insisting on quelling chittavrittis,' Ira said, smiling. '*Tada drashtu svarupe avasthanam*! My gratitude to you, my love, for bringing the Vedanta so close to my heart and mind!'

Adi gently pulled Ira closer to him, kissing her on her forehead. 'May the eternal radiance of the atman shine through you, my dearest!'

Ira trembled slightly in Adi's arms. 'Without you, it would've taken me lifetimes to come this far!'

'How do you know?' Adi asked, smiling at Ira. 'Strange and inscrutable are the ways of the Self!'

A Touch of Shiva

300 Days after the Trek

As Adi walked slowly through the woods, absorbed in meditative silence, he became aware of a vast and luminous presence gathering around him, like a deluge of peace and bliss. It came to him from all directions, from the trees, the ground, the sky. He stood still as the deluge washed over him, filling the pores of his skin with intolerable bliss. A golden stream of light entered his head and brain and descended through his body into the earth beneath. He felt earth itself rising and opening to the sky, as if the last boundary of earth and sky was dissolving in his consciousness. The overwhelming presence engulfed his mind and senses, obliterating the final subtle traces of individuality. Adi's consciousness was now earth and sky, and endless space beyond. But it was no longer Adi's consciousness. It was Shiva everywhere, permeating every form, every movement, in the invisible and the visible, in the felt and the unfelt, in the rise and fall of his own breath, in the movement of the birds, the stirring of the leaves, the rippling breeze and the flowing water.

But this was not the Shiva he had conceived in his higher mind or invoked in his heart, it was not any of the forms humans knew or recognized as Shiva. Shiva was now an intensely conscious and blissful radiance, dense as matter, spread everywhere, which knew itself in the depths of

Adi's being. It was a deep and ancient recall, a wordless understanding that there never was anything else to know.

The trees, fruits and flowers were formed out of Shiva, the breeze was a movement of Shiva, the light of the distant stars were pulsations of Shiva, the ground under his feet was Shiva, his own body and life were emanations of Shiva, his mind was a formation of Shiva, his consciousness itself was Shiva. There was none to invoke and none to be invoked, the last boundary between the finite and the infinite had dissolved in pure bliss, and all that remained was an infinite self-becoming of Shiva.

Adi walked back home, borne by the infinite presence that knew itself as Shiva in all existences, in all forms and movements. This was knowledge that needed no knower. Immutable and absolute.

≈

It was not Ira who awaited him when he reached home—it was Shiva. It was not that Ira had disappeared into Shiva; it was something more miraculous that Adi observed: it was the luminous presence of Shiva that shone through the form he knew so well as Ira. He looked deeper—was this Ira or Shiva? He saw both in a single vision—Ira smiling at him, and Shiva behind the form, smiling at him through her eyes. But who was watching? There was no observer, only the observation, and the whole universe was the observation.

In the lower realm of sense-mind and dualities, where form and name still tugged at the edges of infinite consciousness, Ira stared at Adi's face and eyes, shining with an unearthly radiance, and knew at once that he was no longer the Adi she knew, *her Adi*, the man she loved and wanted to possess more than ever. She knew in her heart, without thought or word, that Adi had passed beyond. She now stood in the compelling presence of a vast and powerful being that she would never know or touch. A deep, unspeakable anguish seared through her heart.

The being that Adi had now become stepped up to her and placed both his hands on her head. Immediately, Ira felt her whole consciousness pulled upward, right into her head, and out of her body through the top of her head. Her physical body, suddenly going limp, fell to the floor like a rag doll. Her consciousness, now free of body and senses, soared upward, opening into the vastness of a luminous space like petals of a flower opening to sunlight.

In the blurred background of her consciousness, Ira felt a being of pure love and light towering over her, his hands on her head. Something or someone deep within her recognized the presence.

'Shiva?' It was a question, but also a tentative recognition.

And Ira awoke to a new day, her whole body trembling uncontrollably with sheer bliss.

Shiva's Cup of Tea

Ira bowed and touched Adi's feet as soon as he emerged from his meditation room that morning.

Adi placed his hand on Ira's head and blessed her. 'Om namah shivaya!'

Ira stood up, her face beaming with joy.

He smiled. 'So, what inspires this devotion today, my dear?'

'You and Shiva came to me in my dream…first you, then Shiva. I felt his hand on my head…it was awesome.'

Adi looked into her eyes. 'You had an inner experience.'

'So, it was not a dream?'

'Your mind processed it as a dream. That often happens.'

'Can we talk about it over tea?' Ira asked eagerly.

'Sure,' Adi replied. 'I'll wait in the garden.'

It was a pleasant morning, with just a few wisps of cloud floating overhead. The peacocks were particularly loud that morning. But Adi loved animal sounds. He could now read animal moods through their sounds, and the reading was getting increasingly accurate. Peacocks were always happy in the mornings, particularly when they could sense rain in the air.

Ira soon joined him with a pot of hot tea and poured each of them a cup.

'Was it real, at some plane?' Ira asked, taking a sip. 'It felt so real!'

'All experiences are real—inner or outer. You must only know how to understand them.'

'Hmm. I remember the dream, or the experience, vividly. You came back from your walk, looking very different... compelling, intense, distant...all of it, actually... and then something happened to me, I felt myself leaving the body... actually saw my body collapse...and then I felt myself rising up into a brightly lit sky...and then you weren't there any more... it was Shiva, I somehow knew that...but he looked so much like you... but much taller, radiant, and there was so much love... and then I woke up with his hands on my head... it felt so real... and then I was awake, trembling all over.'

Both kept quiet after that, slowly sipping their tea. Adi was keenly aware of every movement in Ira's consciousness as she struggled to make sense of her experience.

'Did I really experience Shiva's touch?' Ira asked after several minutes of ruminating. 'His hands on my head? Was he really there?'

'Yes, Ira, you did feel Shiva's touch,' Adi replied. 'But remember, Shiva is pure consciousness, not a person. So, what you saw and felt in your experience was a formation of your own consciousness.'

'Then it was all my own imagination, my own creation?'

'No, it was Shiva alright, but Shiva using your own consciousness to assume a form that would have meaning and significance for you.'

Ira looked hard at Adi, trying to grasp. 'That is why he looked so much like you?'

'Shiva is formless,' Adi continued. 'But he can assume any form—man or woman, devi or deva, human or divine—to manifest to you, in inner or even outer experience.'

'That is how his devotees see him, in a form that makes sense to the devotee?'

'Yes. Mostly, it is a religious and cultural thing. There are all those images and statues of Shiva which devotees internalize.'

'But no one ever sees Shiva as Shiva is,' remarked Ira.

'No one *sees* Shiva, Ira, for the simple reason that there is no physical form to be seen—Shiva is beyond the senses.'

'So, no one will *know* Shiva as Shiva is?'

'Shiva is all-consciousness, all existence, all that can ever be known, in whatever form or forms, the knower and the known. So, in one sense, Shiva is the only thing that can ever be known, and in another sense, Shiva is the unknowable, avyakta.'

It took a while for Ira to grasp that. 'So, the question is not whether anyone will ever know Shiva but whether anyone will ever know anyone or anything else but Shiva.'

Ira continued to drink her tea in silence. Time seemed to stand still.

Then Ira broke the silence. 'But if no one else can be known, how would an Ira know an Adi?'

Adi took a sip of tea. 'That's the play of the mind and senses. If you look deep enough, beyond the memories, projections and constructs of the mind, you will find that there is no Ira or Adi at all. When you are in deep sakshi-bhav, do you still identify yourself as Ira?'

'No, then Ira seems superficial and unreal. I am only witnessing then.'

'Precisely. So, in the real sense, no one knows anyone. All we can know are projections and constructs of the mind, chittavrittis.'

'And when chittavrittis cease, what remains is pure self, pure consciousness, *swarupa*. That swarupa is Shiva, the eternal self!' Ira whispered, sitting motionless with the cup of tea in her hand. 'I am Shiva when I cease to be all that I am not!'

Minutes passed like that, with neither of them moving.

'The tea is getting cold!' Adi said, breaking gently into her thoughts.

Ira almost started. *Tea? What tea? Oh, the tea!* She looked blankly at him. *Why ask about the tea now?*

'If you can keep your attention on the tea while you hold Shiva in your consciousness, you would have attained the balance of yogic dhyana.' Adi whispered, as if sharing a secret. 'If you cannot sense Shiva in the tea, of what good use is the knowledge of Shiva?'

'Shiva in the tea?' Ira repeated, as a deeper understanding dawned. 'In other words, Shiva in all things, in all beings, in all experiences, even the most mundane, the most ordinary—that is a complete yoga!'

Adi nodded, smiling. 'So, do you now understand that once you are conscious of Shiva's presence in your heart, you are practically living with him everywhere and in everything. He can touch you from anywhere, in any form.'

Ira finished her tea in silence. 'I have no questions anymore,' she said. 'And the tea is finished too!'

Rain, Thunder and Emptiness

It was a downpour that evening. Ira and Adi were inside the living room, looking out into the garden from their picture window, enjoying the sound and the sight of the heavy rain.

'I have some wine,' Ira stated, staring into the rain. 'Was wondering…'

Adi turned to her and smiled. 'Let's have a drink.'

Ira stood up. 'Great! Perfect weather for wine!'

She returned in a while with two glasses and a bottle of wine. She poured a drink first for Adi and then for herself. 'Om namah shivaya!' Ira said, smiling.

'Om namah shivaya!' Adi repeated, raising his glass to hers.

Ira took a sip of the wine. 'It's been a while, hasn't it?'

Adi nodded, taking a sip. The wine was good.

'Do you still enjoy these little pleasures, Adi?' Ira asked.

Adi smiled, taking another sip, obviously savouring the wine. 'Well, I've not become an ascetic so far!'

'Don't you become one after taking to yoga?'

'I think that depends on the prakriti, the innate tendencies of one's nature.'

'Is asceticism not mandatory for yoga?'

'I wouldn't know. At least for me it wasn't. I think the one indispensable condition for the yoga would be renunciation of ego and desire. Without that, one cannot proceed on the path.'

'Indispensable?' Ira repeated. 'I would think that kind of renunciation would be an attainment! It's not easy to get rid of ego and desire straight away.'

'Renunciation doesn't have to mean getting rid of something, it's more to do with rejection or refusal, a firm and clear giving up. If it's done sincerely, the thing drops off.'

'Yes, I find that happening with the ego—I'm perfectly aware of the ego in me, when and how it manifests, but I can step back from it, not indulge it.'

'Yes, that is very much possible in the sakshi bhav—you can be aware of a thing without identifying with it or consenting to it. That often works better than struggling and wrestling.'

'Where are you with the ego, Adi? I mean after self-realization, does the ego still survive?'

Adi took a longer sip. 'Ego is a psychological construct, Ira, not a real thing, think of it as an image cast by the atman on the screen of the mind. The moment self-realization dawns, all images and shadows disappear.'

'What about desires?' Ira asked. 'Do they also disappear with self-realization?'

'Desire for an object arises only when the consciousness is identified with that object,' Adi replied. 'After self-realization, the consciousness identifies only with atman.'

Ira thought for a while. 'So, when you are identified with atman, can you still enjoy the world—a drink with the woman you love, a beautiful sunset by the sea, a trek in the mountains?'

Adi smiled. 'The world is not apart from atman, Ira, it is formation of the atman, and atman is all bliss, all delight. What would be the use of anything at all if atman were to be without delight, without bliss?'

'Existence would be dreadfully tedious, dry!'

Adi took a sip of the wine and looked affectionately at Ira. 'You know, one of the Upanishads says this in so many words—*raso vai sah, rasam hyevayam labdhvanandi bhavati*: that which we know as atman or brahman itself is bliss, and attaining to It, one attains all-bliss. In fact, one *becomes* all bliss!'

Ira remembered the sloka. '*Taittiriya Upanishad*,' she said. 'And if this were not so, who would then breathe or live? So, nothing wrong with the desire for rasa, is there?'

'Nothing's wrong with desire. The problem is with identification and attachment. If you get attached to the object of desire, then you fall into moha. Moha keeps you tied to duality. *Yatha rasa, tatha sthiti*—you are, where your rasa is.'

'*Sthiti* refers to state of being?'

'Sthiti comes from the root *stha*, being established. Wherever you find your equilibrium, wherever you're stable.'

'Makes sense. To be established in the highest wisdom, the *sthitaprajna* of the Gita, I must find my rasa in that movement.'

'Yes, in Sanskrit, we say *gati*. Gati means movement. There's a word, *brahmagati*—it means movement towards, or in, brahman.'

'From what I'm understanding, desire is not the issue, the issue is my interest. Obviously, I'll only desire things I'm interested in, and if my sole interest is atman, all other desires will simply disappear—no struggle, no battle!'

'Isn't that logical, Ira?'

Ira nodded while she took a sip of the wine.

'So, in this context, Adi, what is impurity, what the yogis call *asuddhi*?'

'To my mind, from the highest standpoint, duality of any kind would be asuddhi.'

Ira had to strain to listen to Adi's words above the din of the rainfall outside.

'So the only purification needed would be the elimination of duality from one's consciousness?'

'Yes, Ira.'

'And Shiva is pure, non-dual consciousness…'

'Yes, ekam sat.'

'But would there be a world without duality?'

'In truth, there is no world out there—everything we are conscious of is consciousness itself. What we call manifestation is merely self-reflection, Shiva reflecting himself to himself on infinite screens of consciousness, but all one. This is the meaning of Advaita—to know all existence as Shiva and in Shiva, and to know Shiva in all-existence. *Neha nanasti kincana*—there is nothing and no one else.'

'As the Upanishads say, this samsara is a projection of our mind—this is all that we need to understand.'

'The serpent was never there; it was always rope!'

'And then we see Shiva instead of seeing the world?'

'It is all Shiva, the one self, the one atman. Everything in this universe, from the spin of the atom to the movement of the stars, from the first stirrings of life in the cell to the realizations of mahayogis, everything is always pointing back to this one reality.'

Adi's voice was now barely audible, and the sound of the rain outside had become louder. Streaks of lightning flashed across the dark sky and thunders roared in the distance. Ira strained harder to listen.

'Don't strain, Ira. Relax, slow down your breathing. Try to listen with your consciousness.'

Ira slowed down her breathing immediately and, trying no longer to listen to what Adi was saying, she brought all her attention to the quiet space around her head, the *chidakasha*—consciousness-space. And then she heard Adi's voice, clear and firm, chanting right into her ear, quiet and sonorous—

> *Mano buddhi ahankara chittani naaham*
> *na cha shrotra jihve na cha ghrana netre,*
> *na cha vyoma bhumir na tejo na vayuhu,*
> *chidananda rupah shivoham shivoham...*

Who speaks to me then? Who answers my questions? Ira asked wordlessly, knowing Adi was one with her consciousness.

Your own self, Ira—the Self, seated above, the one we call Ishvara. The unspoken words rang though her mind and soul.

Are you that Ishvara? she asked again.

There is only Ishvara, she heard within, *no you or I. Only the Self reflecting the Self. Be quiet and you will know this very instant.*

And the thinking stopped abruptly, and there was only silence.

A silence that drowned out even the storm outside.

≈

Adi and Ira were sitting quietly together, looking out the window. The storm had waned, though it was still drizzling. They could hear the clock in Adi's room faintly chiming midnight.

'I experienced the chidakasha,' Ira said softly. The quietude between them was too precious to break.

'I know,' Adi said quietly. 'Try to station yourself in that space.'

'I can still feel myself there, almost floating.'

'The chidakasha is cosmic.'

'I can only feel it above and around my head.'

'You need to let go of the mental boundaries.'

'They are dissolving...but takes time, doesn't it?'

'Yes, everything takes time, the ignorance is so deeply rooted!'

'I have to go home for a week or so,' Ira said after a while. 'Maybe I'll leave tomorrow.'

'Do that,' said Adi. 'And convey my wishes to your parents.'

'I will,' said Ira. 'Tell me, what happens when I'm not around to pester you with my questions? I mean, what state are you in?'

'Unbroken oneness,' said Adi. 'I'm then in Shiva's cave.'

'Shiva's cave?' Ira asked. 'What, or where, is Shiva's cave?'

'Shiva's cave is a place of unbroken and absolute oneness where even the subtlest universe has dissolved into the Self. Our ancient seers knew this as the cave of the inmost heart, *hridaye guhayam*. It is this cave that is Shiva's sacred abode, the centre of all creation, of all manifestation. There, no vritti arises—mind and heart have subsided into the pure non-dual awareness of Shiva.'

'Where all is resolved into the eternal void, Shiva's shunya?'

'But Shiva's shunya is not void, as in zero, but transcendence, which can perhaps only be described as void.'

'I do not understand transcendence, Adi! I understand zero, the avyakta, and one, the vyakta.'

'Shiva is the transcendence where zero is one, and one is zero, simultaneously.'

'Two quantities being one simultaneously?'

'Neither zero nor one is a measure, Ira; both are dimensions and neither can be measured.'

'And that which transcends these?'

'Transcends dimensions.'

'Dimensionless?'

'Consider the mathematical point that has no dimension yet is the basis for all dimensions.'

'Yes, that I can grasp!'

'That dimensionless point is known as bindu. That bindu is the portal to Shiva's consciousness. When being and becoming, zero and one, avyakta and vyakta—across all dimensions—collapse into dimensionless singularity, it is bindu, or transcendence.'

'Or Shiva?'

'Or Shiva, if you will!'

'Shiva is the transcendence—this I'm beginning to grasp. But how to see the transcendence in the manifest, that I cannot…'

Adi held up two fingers.

'How many fingers do you see?' he asked Ira.

'Two,' Ira replied immediately.

'Close your eyes.'

Ira closed her eyes.

'What would you be seeing if you were never taught language or counting?'

Her mind insisted—*two*.

'Don't think. *Look*. What are you seeing?' Adi asked. 'Just the perception, Ira!'

Ira concentrated, trying to see without thinking. And then, in a flash, she got it. One finger and another finger, not two, but one and one.

'Absolutely!' Adi said, reading her mind. 'You will always *see* one.'

'Yes, one *and* one.'

'Everywhere, in everything. Add, multiply, subtract, divide, you will always see one.'

'The shapes, sizes and kinds may differ?'

'At a gross and empirical scale, yes; at a subtler, quantum scale, even those differences would disappear. But the one would remain.'

'The same one, in all places?'

'Actually, there is only one place, not so many places, as you will soon realize.'

'Only one place? And where is that one place?'

'Here. There is no other place.'

Ira thought for a while. '*Here* would be relative to an object, wouldn't it? For me, this is here but for you, that is here, which for me is there!'

'Yes, but what if I were to remove all objects, all structures, all matter—what would remain?'

'Space…'

'In a sense, yes. If we accept, with the physicists, that spacetime is defined by interactions of matter and energy, then even space would disappear, and what would remain would be the transcendence.'

'The transcendence that is one, and zero, and infinity?'

'Remain with the transcendence, my love. The rest is all conceptual!'

Ira smiled at Adi, a mysterious look in her eyes, and turned towards the window as a flash of lightning streaked across the sky.

Dissolution

The whole universe was floating in Adi's silence. His being was now an oceanic calm that no being or force, within or without, could disturb. Yet, 'within' and 'without' had no relevance in Adi's seamless state of being. He was no longer one person or one being but was everywhere, extended into everything and everyone. All forms and movements, past and present, cosmic and individual, were known to him in an intimacy of consciousness, and all events, from the most distant terrestrial to the most intimately personal, were momentary movements in the expanse of his self-awareness. And in such a state, indescribable in words, he lived day to day.

Though there was neither person nor measured time any more, the sense of person or personhood was now a distant memory of some past lifetime, and the measure or sense of human time was replaced by the inscrutable rhythms of cosmic becomings—births and dissolutions, explosions of consciousness, outpourings of light from fathomless darkness, and scintillating sparks exploding into giant stars, and then falling back into massive implosions of invisible energy.

'Adi' was now just the outer physical shell moved more by karmic momentum than by any defined personal will to live. The body would go about its daily functions efficiently and automatically, with no interference of intention, thought or feeling. The consciousness enveloping and watching over the body would only sometimes, when absolutely needed, intervene and gently rectify whatever needed to be rectified. The physical body was still primitive, still pretty much a creature of habit and tendency.

And then, one night, as Adi lay down to rest his body, he felt an inner loosening, almost a sense of coming apart of the cells of the body. The breathing, already imperceptibly slow, slowly ceased, and the prana withdrew from the physical shell into the universe. The cells of the body, suddenly without a cohesive force binding them into tissues and muscles, drifted away, in slow motion, into cosmic space. The farther the cells drifted, the more Adi felt his physical body becoming fluid, like warm water, flowing away in all directions. The water became warmer and warmer as it floated away and began to turn slowly into fire at its farthest reaches. And then all Adi could feel was fire, not burning but deeply soothing, envelop his whole being, and what was once his body had turned to fire. But the fire kept spreading, farther and farther, till it turned into a warm glowing gaseous cloud, almost a nebula. And then, the gaseous nebula evaporated into luminous space, and nothing of Adi remained.

That night Adi felt one with the universe in the very cells of his body, spread out everywhere, in everything and everyone, beyond all division and duality. He woke up in the middle of the night, completely conscious, no longer in a particular human body but in a body that was at once cosmic, terrestrial and personal, held together in one seamless consciousness.

Not by Yoga Alone

When Ira returned in a few weeks, she found Adi sitting on his chair in the living room, staring fixedly outside the window. She entered the room quietly, very careful not to disturb his quietude, and immediately felt a palpable density in the air around Adi. It took a few moments for Adi to register her presence. She came up to him, bowed low, and touched his feet. He placed his right palm on her head, blessing her silently. The density around Adi seemed overwhelming.

Adi smiled warmly at her. 'Welcome back!' His voice sounded different, perhaps somewhat impersonal, and certainly more resonant. His eyes had the faraway look of a poet, but his face was radiant, perhaps more so than before. She knew instinctively that he had gone far deeper into his yoga during her absence.

'Something about you has changed,' she said a bit uncertainly.

'Yes, the consciousness deepens and heightens all the time. There seems to be no limit.'

'You always said it is infinite.'

Adi smiled. 'Yes, but I had no idea how infinite the infinite can be.'

'But I'm glad I'm back. Seems increasingly difficult to adjust to the world out there. This is my home and my ashram—at your feet, in your presence.'

'You too have deepened; I can feel the silence in your heart.'

'I've been following your instructions to the T. Keeping the mind as concentrated as possible and invoking Shiva in the heart all the time.'

Adi smiled.

'Would you want some tea?' she asked.

'Yes,' Adi said, 'that would be good.'

When Ira returned with the tea, Adi was standing by the window, staring at something outside. As soon as she entered, Adi turned around and came back to his chair. Ira placed the teapot and cups on the table in front of them and sat down on her chair.

'You must have missed the tea!' She said as she poured the tea in the cups.

Adi picked up his cup and sipped his tea slowly and deliberately. 'Yes, I did.'

'Just the tea?' she teased.

Adi chuckled. 'Let's keep it to the tea, shall we?'

'But seriously, you cannot possibly be remembering or missing anything anymore, can you?'

'No, there is no personal memory anymore.'

'One doesn't really need a personal memory. I felt it this time—that most of my memories are useless!'

'Sometimes it is necessary to integrate certain past experiences in the consciousness. It is necessary for the sadhana.'

'No experience to be left unintegrated, everything to be wrapped up?'

'No loose ends, shall we say?'

'No experience or event is trivial from the yogic point of view, right?'

'Nothing is trivial from the yogic point of view. Every experience has its value, and its place.'

'Even the little things we do unconsciously?'

'The thing is to integrate everything that has happened to us, and through us, in a deeper and more luminous understanding.'

'That is why the seers ask us to regard our daily life as sacred!'

'Including the drinking of tea.'

'I remember—Shiva in all things.'

Adi continued sipping his tea.

'There's another thing that keeps coming to me,' Ira said.

Adi turned to face her, smiling. He knew what she was going to ask.

'Why can you not be my guru? Initiate me into your yoga.'

'But I have no yoga of my own.'

'The yoga that is happening through you…'

'The true guru dwells within, Ira, in the cave of your heart.'

'But what about a human guru?'

'The human guru too will lead you to your inner guru.'

'Well, at least do that.'

'Do what?'

'Lead me to my inner guru.'

'But I am doing just that as your sahadharmi. Why on earth would you want me as a guru too?'

'Hmm,' Ira nodded. 'Makes sense. But there's this constant need to know how I am progressing in the sadhana—what to do with that?'

'Old habit of the mind to measure, compare. Pay no attention to any of that—whatever you don't pay attention to, goes away.'

Ira poured herself and Adi another cup of tea.

'Can we talk about something mundane?'

'Mundane?'

'Family matters.'

'Sure.'

'My family wants us to get married. I mean, formally married.'

'Yes, they must be worried about your future.'

'I told them that marriage is not important for either of us, that we are both involved in yoga.'

'Do they understand yoga?'

'Well, they have some quaint ideas about it. For instance, the idea that yogis live in ashrams, and don't have personal relations, and most of them are escapists. Things like that, you know.'

Adi smiled. 'Yes, I know. These are mostly unexamined, stereotypical ideas.'

Ira smiled. 'There's a lot of scepticism!'

'That's understandable. But what about you? Does the thought of marriage come to you?'

'You can read me better,' Ira said. 'What do you feel?'

'Well, when we are together, you don't think of marriage at all.'

'You are right,' Ira said thoughtfully. 'When I'm with you, the marriage vritti does not arise. In fact, a lot of other vrittis don't arise. Even the sex vritti disappears when I'm with you, not a trace, whereas logically, it should be the strongest when I'm with you!'

That made Adi smile. 'What you say is true—most vrittis will disappear in my presence.'

'Something to do with the yoga?'

'Because you are psychically open to me.'

'They say that the fruits of a rishi's tapasya are automatically transferred to his sahadharmi—is that true?'

'Yes, it is.'

'Is that what is happening with me?'

'I would think so.'

'That is extraordinary!' Ira remarked.

'What's so extraordinary about it? Isn't it natural?'

'I suppose so, we all affect each other, even in the ordinary life. The effect of a Yogi's field will be that much more!'

'I can think of Ramkrishna and Ma Sharada. He transferred the spiritual consciousness to her directly. And he did that with some others too, including Vivekananda.'

'But that does not, of course, mean that I can take my sadhana for granted?'

Adi shrugged. 'Who knows how it all works!'

Ira smiled. 'You would know, wouldn't you?'

Adi smiled back but did not respond.

Ira chuckled softly. 'Sometimes you're quite unfathomable! But then, I'm getting a bit enlightened too!'

'That you are, my dear!' Adi said. 'That you are.'

'Shall we have something to eat?' Ira asked.

'Why not? Thou shalt not live by yoga alone!'

Shiva in All Things

Adi was pacing meditatively back and forth in his room when Ira came in. He stopped momentarily when he saw her.

'Am I disturbing?' she asked.

Adi didn't tell her that he was already aware that she was going to step into his room at exactly the moment she stepped in.

'Not at all,' he replied, smiling.

He also didn't tell her that he knew what she wanted to discuss.

'I wanted to know more about identification with Shiva.'

He sat down on his couch. 'You have a question?'

'What exactly identifies with Shiva?'

'The identification is already there. Only the veils are removed.'

'The veils of mind and ego?'

'Yes. The mind and ego are superimposed just as the serpent, in the popular Vedantic analogy, is superimposed on the rope.'

'Adhyaropa?'

'Yes. And when the veils are removed, Shiva shines through. Then the identification is realized.'

'Knowledge by identity?'

'Yes.'

'And, at the moment of the realization, the I will cease to exist.'

'Yes.'

'So, there will be no I-thought in the identification?'

'No.'

'Then who is there to say *shivoham*—I am Shiva?'

'Shivoham is not a thought, it is not something one says or thinks to oneself, or to anyone else.'

'Shivoham, not a thought?'

'It is a knowing. You just know it.'

'I don't understand.'

'You know you are Ira right now, don't you?'

'Yes.'

'Do you need to think or say that to yourself?'

'No. But I may need to say it to you, in some context.'

'Sure. But when I'm not there?'

'Then, no.'

'And if Ira were to be the only living being in the universe?'

'Then there would be no context or reason at all.'

'And if the universe itself was Ira?'

'Then even I wouldn't be there. There would be only Ira.'

'And what would that Ira know?'

'Ira.'

'And that Ira would be known only to Ira, in absolute self-identity, no subject, no object, no duality. That is identification. When only Shiva is, and none other.'

Ira sat down quietly facing Adi.

'And then there is no one to think shivoham.'

'Absolute identification, the end of knowledge.'

'But where does the world go then?'

'Nowhere. The world is a formation in Shiva. When mind rests in Shiva, the world no longer distracts—it's just there, like a song in the background.'

'Why does this song in the background exist at all? For what purpose, what reason?'

'The human mind needs purpose or significance, Shiva has no such need, it exists for itself and by itself. *Svayambhu*—self-manifested, self-existent.'

'We just need to remove the namarupa filters from our mind, and then we will see that there is only one thing, one truth, and everything points only to that.'

'Yes, precisely.'

Ira kept quiet for a long time. Adi remained seated on his couch, unmoving.

'The buddhi must live without names, without labels, without the need to describe anything,' Ira remarked.

'Yes, and when mind begins to perceive without mental filters of names, measures and descriptions, it attains purity, suddhi.'

'The purification from *bhedbhav*, the sense of differentiation.'

'Yes, the buddhi passes beyond bhedbhav.'

≈

Later that afternoon, while strolling through the woods, Adi pointed to a tree and asked Ira, 'What do you see?'

Ira looked at the tree. The mental description was immediate. She was seeing a tree—branches, leaves, flowers, and then she reminded herself that she was not actually seeing a tree, she was thinking a tree, she was thinking branches, leaves, flowers.

'The buddhi recognizes this as a tree,' she replied, weighing every word. 'Yet, what I perceive is a form which has no name, no description.'

'Can you sense the buddhi superimposing the tree-construct on this form?'

'It happens almost automatically.'

'But it can be slowed, made more conscious, the adhyaropa habit can be broken.'

Ira stood still, watching the tree and trying to perceive it without the construct of tree.

'It may be a bit difficult to begin with,' Adi explained. 'The perception is deeply conditioned by the intellect. It takes a lot of concentration to purify the perception.'

'Pure perception is to see a thing as it is?'

'To see not *a* thing but *the* thing.'

'Meaning?'

'Perception without bhedbhav—not this thing, this person here or that thing, that person there but one thing, one being, one movement, everywhere.'

'One thing, one being, without name, without description, without differentiation…'

'Yes, Ira. Can you?'

'I can, let me try. Can I do this while walking?'.

'You can only do this while walking. You must be dynamically engaged with prakriti to see through her, to see her without her veils of namarupa.'

'This will include you as well, Adi—not to see you as Adi the namarupa but as pure consciousness, as Shiva.'

'It will start with yourself, to regard yourself as Shiva, and not the Ira namarupa.'

'And then we shall find Shiva in all things, Shiva in all beings?'

'Indeed, my dear. And, by Shiva's grace, may that realization come to you. Om!'

'Om!' Ira repeated softly.

Identification

Ira woke up that morning with a clarity she had never known before, as if her whole being had lit up from within. Her body was suffused with deep peace and joy. She had never experienced such deep joy with such solid peace before. She knew at once that something important was happening in Adi, and an essence of whatever was happening, in some mysterious way, was transferring directly to her mind and body. Sensing her own inner state, she could tell that Adi was reaching some still higher realization in his being.

She quickly made some tea for Adi and herself and went over to his room. As soon as she came up to the door, which was closed, she could feel an almost physical intensity around her. She was debating whether to enter his room when she distinctly felt him nudging her to come inside. She opened the door carefully and stepped in.

She gasped when she saw him. He was seated on his couch, erect and motionless, eyes closed, his body glowing from within. There was a dense silence in the room which she could feel on her skin and inside her head. She felt her mind instantly fall into deep silence.

She tiptoed towards him and placed the cups of tea before him on the table, careful not to disturb the intense silence of the room. She then sat down on the floor before him and felt her eyes closing by themselves. For a few moments she was aware of his presence, overwhelming her senses, and then she lost all awareness of space and time.

After what seemed a few moments only, she felt a gentle nudge inside her again and she slowly opened her eyes. Adi was looking at her, a soft smile playing about his lips. His skin was still aglow with an inner light, and the silence around him was still as dense. It did not feel that she was in a man's presence, it seemed as if she was looking at one of the devas, the luminous ones, of old. She bowed her head involuntarily.

Then Adi's voice, ever so soft and gentle, floated into her head. 'Ira, the identification with Shiva is now complete.'

Ira could understand the words, but the implication completely escaped her. She knew what identification with Shiva meant, Adi had explained that to her on several occasions. But this was something altogether different. She could sense it in her bones. *What did this mean? Was she sitting in Shiva's presence, then? But Shiva is formless—nirakara rupo. Yet, the one she knew and loved as Adi—the consciousness in the form—had identified with Shiva, so had indeed become Shiva, for isn't identification self-becoming?* She looked up at him, not giving voice to her thoughts, sure that he was reading her more clearly than ever.

'You will know,' he said aloud. His voice was somehow softer than usual, as if coming from a great inner distance. 'You don't have to think, the understanding will come from Shiva.'

As he said the words, she felt the glow from his skin enveloping her body and senses. At once, her whole being was filled with a peace she had never imagined possible, a peace that was at once outside and inside her being, penetrating her very cells and simultaneously radiating outward from her cells into open space. And then, Ira saw, or inwardly sensed, a single ray of light emanating from Adi and entering her head. Immediately, all thinking in her mind ceased, all thoughts disappeared, and her whole consciousness fell into a deep and dense silence. Her eyes closed of themselves as she felt her body sinking into an indescribable velvety softness which enveloped her completely.

Later that night, they sat together in the living room, in silence, and shared a bowl of vegetable soup. Ira had switched off the electric lights and had lit two earthen lamps, which Adi always preferred. After nearly an hour, Adi got up, went to his room, and returned with a cigar. He opened the window and lit the cigar. Ira came up and stood quietly beside him, looking outside into the starlit night. The peace around Adi was solid, palpable, and she was herself steeped in that peace, her mind thoughtless, empty. She knew that she had crossed a threshold of her being.

≈

Ira woke up next morning with the sound of Om resonating across her bedroom. She sat up on her bed, her mind still empty, motionless. As she concentrated, she realized that the sound of Om was not in the physical space around her but inside her own being. The sound was deep, soft, soothing. She closed her eyes, and let herself sink into the vibration of Om, rising from one syllable into another and then spreading cosmically into the hum of the final syllable. The deeper she sank into the vibration, the denser and more luminous the sound became. The sound and the light were one, yet neither sound nor light. The whole universe, in its subtlest essence, was this sound and light, one merging fathomlessly into the other like an ocean falling in slow motion into another ocean. And everything, everywhere was conscious of everything, everywhere. The understanding came on its own, without thought or word. Or perhaps, it did not come, it was always there, in the fabric of the universe that Ira—or what used once to be Ira—had now become.

The universe is not outside of us, nor is it inside. There is indeed no inside or outside. The universe is what we are, it is what we endlessly become. All thought of difference is illusion. There is only one existence, one reality. It is to this one reality we give the name Shiva. Or brahman. Or God. But what is the big deal with words? Or with language itself? That which is, is forever beyond thought and word. Forever unknowable to our human consciousness. To know that which is, our human consciousness itself has to expand, evolve, rise higher, go deeper, into itself. This is the eternal odyssey of the great seers of old. But what 'old'? Time itself is an illusion. When consciousness passes beyond time, we realize that there is no old or new, everything is here and now. The ancient seers are still within us, living in and through us, bearing in their fathomless silence the vicissitudes of our existence in space and time. We are, despite all appearances, one. Indivisibly one.

And to know that we are that one existence, everywhere, in everything, in everyone, is to know the secret of secrets. That is evolution of consciousness. To seek, to know, and to grow. For there is no end to seeking, no end to knowing.

Yogas chittavritti nirodha.
Tada drashtu svarupe avasthanam.

For Swami Vivekananda

II

Kalki and the First Awakening

Kalki

A vast cosmic presence watched over Kalki as she sat rock still in a profound yogic trance, her consciousness descending, like a slow vortex of silver light, ever deeper into a fathomless abyss of velvety darkness. And as her consciousness descended, layer by layer, into that dark abyss, she remembered, in the very depths of her soul, a cry that none had heard, none heeded, for there was none to hear or heed—that one searing memory that had become the seeding of endless future becomings, for every universe is born out of the embers of the last one, and the anguish of death in one turns to the ecstasy of birth in another. This is the great continuity of existence: one single thread running through all cosmos, binding the quark to the galaxy, the protoplasm to the maharshi. What seems empty cosmic space is but the invisible web of infinite becomings.

≈

Kalki had chosen to remain human, though she could have been an entire world—a *loka*—by herself; she could have been a godhead, above and beyond forms, even the vastest, but she had chosen and willed to remain human. It is in the human world that she had found the possibility of redemption, and of final fulfilment. That which still yearned in her for endless life, for immortality.

≈

She stood alone at her window looking out into a world that she barely recognized, a world whose fate still hung by a delicate thread, swinging pendulum-like between light and life, and decay and dissolution, a world that still aspired for godhead but sank ever deeper into the gathering darkness of the primeval *tamas*. *Would Mira break the impasse, cross the threshold and make that difference*—Kalki wondered without thought. For there was no knowledge yet of the coming hours, just a lone and silent aspiration living deep in the heart of things. Kalki realized, yet again, how much depended on her own will, her own strength, to overcome the last surge of the tamas, the irresistible pull downward into dissolution. She knew the pull well now, it was something she lived with by the hour, the mesmerizing pull of death, the inflexible law of entropy. And there was no escape, not even for one like her.

It was in her being—made cosmic through lifetimes of tapasya—that the final battle was raging, ocean swells of tamas pushing back against the onslaught of Light, Light that should have by now impregnated the timeless dark. But with every swell, she only grew more prayerful, more surrendered—for this was her purpose, the reason for her birth in time.

≈

'Tamas has entered my very bones,' she had confided in Krishna one summer night many ages ago. 'I do not know how long this body will last…'

Krishna had replied, holding her hand lovingly in his, 'Tamas must be overcome in the body, Kalki, in the very heart of matter. It is not in consciousness, even the highest, that it can be done.'

'But the tamas gets heavier…' she had said, looking deep into Krishna's soul, her eyes reflecting the weariness of the body, eyes that had once blazed with fierce shakti. And looking into his soul, she had quietly prayed for rest, for release.

Krishna had held her gaze, his very being pouring itself into Kalki, and his words penetrating the dense fog of her weariness. 'Not yet, Kalki, not yet. If you give up now, the battle will be lost again, everything will be pushed back by centuries!'

'But the resistance…'

'I know, I know how the resistance grows stronger, more obdurate. But that is the sign, Kalki, that the battle has gone down into the body. And it is there that you must overcome it.'

Kalki had understood what she had known through the centuries. The densest darkness would precede the breaking of dawn…

'Will you be with me this time, Krishna?' she had asked.

But her question was more of a prayer. She wanted Krishna to be with her. Without him, she would fall apart.

'I will!' Krishna had promised. He knew the stakes were higher this time.

'Then give me strength,' Kalki had prayed again to the mighty soul towering over her consciousness. 'Give me the strength to withstand…'

And Krishna had given her the force, the strength, by pouring all his shakti into her being, into the very cells of her body, and Kalki's soul and body had drunk thirstily of Krishna's shakti that poured into her like flowing nectar. Krishna had then assured her, his words seeping into her soul, 'You, Kalki, shall carry forth the Light that I have seeded in you—in you, and through you, my shakti shall work upon this earth till all is done!'

She had known then, in a single lightning flash of consciousness, that Mira would tilt the scales.

Mira

Mira was six years old when the first experience came. Her parents had taken her to a hill station for a holiday. They were staying at a hotel that had a beautiful garden right outside. Mira was playing in that garden when she saw this beautiful bright blue butterfly on a white flower. The tiny fluttering spot of bright blue on the white flower fascinated little Mira. She tiptoed towards it. The butterfly flew off. Mira gave chase. The butterfly led little Mira out of the hotel gate and on to the road outside. Her attention riveted on the butterfly, and she started running across the road. At that very moment, just a few meters from her, a car turned onto the road, speeding towards her. Mira caught the movement from the corner of her eye. And then it all happened in a flash. As the car came up speeding, a force seized her body and threw her clean across the road. Mira could feel the car whiz past her as she rolled softly on to the grassy ground beside the road. She stood up quickly, unhurt but shaken. She didn't want to attract any attention to herself. The last thing she wanted was to be told by her mother not to go out to play by herself. She ran back into the hotel and, once inside, she looked around—had anyone noticed? Apparently, no one had. Relieved, she walked back into the hotel building.

That night, lying on her bed, staring up at the ceiling, she thought again about what had happened. She could vividly recall being seized by something and hurled across the road, and the feeling of landing on a kind of cushion across the road. Two questions arose in her mind that night—what or who had thrown her across the road? And how did she not feel any hurt when she landed on the ground across the road? Even to her six-year-old mind, this was not normal. She wished she could ask her mother these questions, but she also knew she wouldn't.

≈

In another dimension, separated not by space or time but by a luminous veil of consciousness, a man and a woman stood in the starlit night looking at Mira's sleeping form on the bed in the hotel room. Both were very tall, and their bodies softly luminous, as if clothed in light.

'She is safe,' the man said to the woman, his voice deep and gentle.

The woman nodded. 'But it was a close call.'

'Agreed,' he said. 'We should be more vigilant now.'

The woman looked carefully, probingly, at Mira's body on the bed across the veil.

'When does she become conscious?' she asked.

'Not until she turns eight,' the man replied quietly. 'If all goes well, that is!'

'But with Krishna himself watching, what can go wrong?'

'Krishna only watches, he does not intervene.'

'But there is hope, now that she's back.'

The man turned briefly to face the woman. They looked at each other. She understood, words were not needed.

≈

In the earth dimension, but beyond the threshold of human consciousness, veiled by her own force, Kalki too stood by the window of her cottage, looking intently at Mira. Kalki knew in her heart who and what Mira was, but she couldn't yet bring that knowledge to surface, even in herself. The time was not ripe. There was still much to be prepared. But Kalki could sense something deeper stirring in Mira's being, and she wondered if it would happen earlier. The outer conditions on earth were still unstable, and the resistance was growing, which she could feel in her body now. Her body, already over three hundred years old, was beginning to show the strain of the almost continuous struggle against death. But she also knew that the victory was assured—Mira was alive and growing.

Kalki kept gazing at Mira in her yogic vision as Mira lay fast asleep on her bed in her corner of the universe. She knew, even as she gazed upon her, that through her gaze, Sri Krishna himself was watching over the little girl. An old nameless memory stirred in her heart.

≈

Mira was sitting in the corner of her classroom, her crayon clutched in her hand, her eyes tightly shut. She was concentrating hard on how to draw a tiger. She could recall a tiger in her mind's eye, but she was not getting the eyes right. The eyes, as her art teacher had told the class, is the most important thing. But for some reason, she was unable to focus. She was sensing something unpleasant in her immediate atmosphere and didn't know what it was. She opened her eyes and looked around. There was a commotion in the corridor outside the classroom and all her classmates were jostling at the door. Everyone seemed excited. She too got up and walked up to the door.

A tall and sturdy boy, quite certainly a senior, was towering over one of her classmates, a small boy they all used to call Jo. She was particularly fond of Jo as he was the only one in the class who used to share all his fancy crayons and games with her. Mira could now clearly sense that the unpleasantness was coming at her in waves from the senior who was standing threateningly over Jo. She didn't like the senior doing whatever he was doing to Jo. And she could also sense that Jo was afraid of the big bully.

Mira closed her eyes, clenching her fists. She clearly saw Jo and the bully inside her head, and she put herself into Jo's body, effortlessly, as if she had done such a thing a thousand times. Then she straightened out Jo's cowering body, standing up tall to the bully, suddenly looking him in the eye. The bully instinctively took a step back. Jo placed his right hand against the bully's chest and, with a surge of strength from within, pushed him back. The bully, with all his size and strength, went hurtling across the corridor, crashing against the opposite wall.

Suddenly, all the children froze and there was pin drop silence for a few seconds. Quite dazed, the senior boy stood up, feeling the bump on his head. He stared unbelievingly at Jo. An inexplicable fear seized his heart, and he turned away and walked off as quickly as his feet could carry him. Jo, too, stared, equally unbelievingly, at the senior's receding back, unable to figure out what had just happened. When he turned around, all his classmates erupted in loud cheers, attracting the attention of the teachers in the other classrooms. Jo walked back into the class, feeling elated, smiling like a hero. Then he spotted Mira, standing still, looking straight at him. He smiled at her. She kept staring right through him. For some reason he couldn't comprehend, she looked very strange.

That night, while her parents slept in their bedroom adjoining hers, Mira sat awake on her bed, contemplating the event at school. Something had happened—she had somehow got into Jo's body.

≈

The tall man was observing Mira's sleeping body on the other side, probing gently into her mind, when the woman joined him. She stood quietly beside him for a few moments and then spoke to him, almost in a whisper: 'She is beginning to unravel, Oja. Something is accelerating the process.'

'We don't know enough,' the one called Oja replied. 'It may be a natural process of awakening. Let's observe a while longer. If this keeps happening—or accelerating, as you say—we may need to call for intervention.'

'Agreed,' she said. 'I will keep a watch.'

He nodded and, turning, walked away quietly.

The woman continued watching Mira as she slept. Like Oja, she too had the power of subtle vision and could probe the inner workings of the mind. She saw that Mira was in deep sleep, her inmost being gathered, like a dense light, in the psychic. She offered Mira silently to Krishna and closed her eyes.

So far, Mira was safe and sound.

≈

Mira was still asleep when she became aware of Oja and the woman. She saw both standing before her, on some kind of raised platform, looking intently at her. Mira stared back, without any kind of fear or apprehension. She was curious, though, and asked them who they were. Neither of them, it seemed, could hear her. They were engrossed in their own conversation which Mira couldn't hear. When Mira observed a bit more closely, she noticed that both people were unusually tall, she had never seen anyone so tall before. She also noticed that they were standing in the open and there were lots of bright stars in the sky. Suddenly, she recalled the nursery rhyme she had learnt some time ago—*twinkle, twinkle little star*. But the stars were not little, they were big and bright and were not twinkling at all.

When she woke up the next morning, all Mira remembered were the big and bright stars in the sky and someone singing *twinkle, twinkle little star* to her.

The memory of what had happened in school that morning was still very vivid in her mind. She felt bad about hurting that senior, although she felt that he had deserved it—he had no right to bully Jo. But what she couldn't figure out was how it had all happened—how had she got into Jo, how had she thrown off the bully with such strength? She decided on a whim to talk to the only person she trusted enough among the adults with such matters: her father.

Her father was a writer and would be working away at his computer almost through the day. Occasionally, he would get out of his study to take a break. Then he would play with Mira if she was at home or go for a walk if she was not. In the evenings, her father and mother would go for walks together. That morning her father was taking a tea break when she came into his study. This was the time he would sit back and enjoy the tea her mother would make for him.

'Yes, sweetheart?' her father said, planting a kiss on her forehead. 'What can I do for my precious?'

'I have something to discuss,' Mira said gravely, using the phrase she had often heard her parents use whenever they needed to talk about serious matters.

Her father immediately looked serious too. 'Of course. Please have a seat, young lady!'

She pulled out the small chair kept for her in a corner and sat down on it, facing her father. Her father pushed aside his keyboard, placed his glasses on the table, and waited for her to speak. She liked the way her father would always listen to her, with complete attention. She felt like a grown up.

She related to him the entire incident with Jo and the bully. 'I'm sorry that I had to hurt him,' she concluded, feeling a lot better now that she had shared it all with her father.

Her father closed his eyes and sat back. He had heard her out carefully. He knew that his daughter was not given to exaggeration or fabrication, a child who would not make up stories even to save herself from trouble. A virtue, he believed, she had inherited from her mother, Esha.

'Has this kind of a thing ever happened before, Mira?' he asked after some time, looking carefully at his daughter.

'No, dad…' she paused, hesitant. He caught her hesitation immediately.

'Something else you wish to tell me, Mira?' he asked gently.

Mira thought. It would be best to share the other incident too. She may get a scolding for having strayed out of the hotel alone, but it was something that needed to be shared.

'Dad, I did something which you and Ma may not like,' she began, and then paused.

Her father leaned forward on the table and said as gently as he could, 'Mira, my child, there is nothing that we won't like. You are a very wise child, and we trust you!'

'When we went to that hotel in Darjeeling,' she said.

Her father nodded. 'Yes, last year. What happened?'

'I was chasing a butterfly, dad…and I went out of the hotel running after it.'

Her father recalled the setting. 'Yes, there was a road outside.'

'And a car came up…speeding at me.'

His heart skipped a beat. He kept quiet, not wanting to interrupt.

'And something took hold of me, dad, and threw me to the other side.'

'Threw you? On the sidewalk across the road?'

'Yes, dad! And I wasn't hurt at all. I landed on something very soft.'

'Something took hold of you, Mira?'

'Yes, like…someone…or something…'

'And you didn't tell Ma, or me?'

Mira looked down. How could she? 'I'm sorry, dad…'

He smiled at her. 'It's okay, darling. Doesn't matter. Thank God you were safe. Next time, you must be more careful!'

'I will, dad.' Mira promised. But inside her head, there was another thought that she couldn't shake off.

≈

Once Mira had gone to sleep that night, her parents sat together in the lawn outside their house.

Esha looked worried, uncertain. 'She doesn't exaggerate,' she said quietly to her husband.

'Exactly what I thought when she first told me,' he said. 'There's no reason to disbelieve her.'

'No, I'm not disbelieving her—it's something else I'm worried about, Som,' she said looking at him. 'How can we be sure it's not all in her head?'

Som narrowed his eyes. This hadn't struck him at all.

'I spoke to her art teacher,' Esha continued. 'And she told me about this incident. That boy Jo was being bullied by a senior when he suddenly stood up to him and threw the senior against the opposite wall.'

'Yes, just as she told me.'

'And everyone was quite amazed that Jo could do what he did. Jo is about half the size of the senior. The senior studies in eighth grade.'

'So, not a very likely thing to happen?' Som asked his wife.

'No. But then, with kids, you never know,' Esha replied.

'But how much more likely is Mira's version?'

'That she got *into* Jo and threw off the senior? Highly unlikely. Jo suddenly and somehow getting that kind of strength is not so unlikely: unlikely things happen when anger or frustration builds up over time. I checked—Jo and that senior student have had their tiffs before. That senior is a known bully.'

'Hmm,' Som nodded. 'And about the car incident? How does one explain that?'

'But no one else saw that happen, Som,' Esha said quietly. 'No one at the hotel. Otherwise, someone or the other would've told us. And think about it—after such an incident, which can shake just about anyone up, our daughter told us nothing!'

'And you didn't sense anything out of place either,' Som added. 'Which any mother would have, immediately.'

Esha nodded in agreement. 'Which is what makes me think…'

She didn't complete her sentence. It hung between them: *it's all in her imagination*.

'But it is normal for children her age to have such a vivid imagination,' Som said after a long pause.

'Yes, it is,' Esha agreed, 'but as long as imagination is not mistaken for reality.'

Som stood up and stretched himself. He was sensing a knot in his stomach. He let out a long breath. 'Esha,' he said, 'let's not give this too much importance. Let's wait and see. If more such incidents happen, we will discuss again. Meanwhile, we just underplay this with Mira.'

'Yes, agreed,' Esha said, slightly relieved. 'Want a drink?'

'Yes, I need one!' Som said, smiling.

≈

Mira dreamt that night.

Her parents were sitting outside on the lawn, looking worried. She was sitting on the patio steps playing with a blue butterfly, the kind she had been chasing at the hotel. Her mother came up to her. The butterfly stopped fluttering and sat quietly on her knee.

'Mira, my child,' her mother leaned down to her and whispered in her ear. 'There are things that you do not discuss with anyone.'

Mira looked up at her mother. 'Not even you and dad, Ma?'

'No, my child. Grown-ups don't understand everything that happens to children,' she said.

'Ma, are you upset with me?' Mira asked.

'Not at all, Mira,' her mother said reassuringly. 'Nor dad. We love you.'

Mira smiled. 'What happens to this butterfly, Ma? Can I keep it?'

'This is a magical butterfly, isn't it?' her mother asked, looking closely at the butterfly.

The butterfly was glowing in a deep blue light. It looked bigger than before. And it was looking straight at Mira. Mira looked into its eyes and asked, 'Are you magical?'

'I come from fairyland,' the butterfly replied. It had a small squeaky voice.

'See, it even speaks!' Her mother was laughing.

'Where's fairyland, butterfly?' Mira asked.

'Everywhere, Mira,' the butterfly replied. 'All around you. But people don't see it.'

'Can I see it?' Mira asked again.

'Yes, if you want to, little one!'

Mira started laughing. 'Look, Ma—it is calling *me* the little one!'

Her mother laughed again. 'Does it have a name?'

'Do you have a name, butterfly?' Mira asked, looking at the butterfly.

'My friends call me Buffy,' the butterfly said and fluttered her bright blue wings.

'Can I meet your friends?' Mira asked.

'If they want to meet you,' Buffy said and fluttered her wings again.

The fluttering of the butterfly's wings woke Mira up. She opened her eyes and looked around. It was still dark. Everything was quiet around her. Buffy was still on her mind. She smiled and closed her eyes. Her mother's words floated across her consciousness as she drifted off to sleep again—*Grown-ups don't understand everything that happens to children*.

≈

A year later, Mira had her first yogic experience. Exactly seven days after her seventh birthday.

Mira remembered that day clearly: the school had invited a monk from the local ashram to teach the children how to meditate. Mira had no idea what meditation meant but for some reason, she was excited. She was always excited at the prospect of learning something new.

As soon as the morning assembly was over, the head mistress invited the monk on stage. A sudden hush descended in the spacious hall. Almost the whole school was there. The monk was short, quite bald, and looked chubby from a distance. Mira liked him instantly: he reminded her of a teddy bear. She chuckled at the thought.

'My dear children,' the head mistress began. 'As I promised, we have Swami Nityananda with us today who will teach us meditation! Swamiji has worked a lot with children like yourselves, all over India, teaching them to meditate. I'm very sure that you will all enjoy learning from him!'

There was a subdued applause as the Swami stepped in front of the microphone.

The Swami folded his hands and did namaskar to the students and teachers assembled in the hall. Everyone present also returned the gesture.

'Has anyone here heard of meditation?' the Swami asked, looking at the children seated in the front few rows. The teachers, seated in the rows behind, kept quiet. A few hands went up, especially among the senior students. The Swami picked one of the students and asked her to respond.

'You close your eyes,' the student said, 'and breathe deeply.'

'Good,' said the Swami. 'And then?'

'Then?' The student thought for a few seconds. 'Then you breathe deeply!'

Some of the students tittered. The Swami smiled. 'That's alright,' he said gently. 'Not too many people know what happens after that. That is the reason I am here this morning. To see if anything else happens after you close your eyes and breathe deeply.'

He had everyone's attention. The younger children, particularly.

'So, we will all close our eyes,' the Swami declared. He himself closed his eyes, and the rest of the audience followed. There was complete silence in the hall. 'Now, with your eyes closed, you will listen to my voice...I will chant Om three times, and you can all repeat after me.'

After a few seconds, the Swami's voice rose, chanting Om. The entire hall resonated with the chanting as the teachers and the students followed.

It was during the second chant that Mira's mind blanked out completely. One moment, she was aware of sitting on her chair in the school hall, chanting Om. The next moment, it was all gone—the hall, the school, the chanting, the children. She was floating in open space, and there were blue and golden streaks of lightning all around her. Before she could react to what was happening, she saw a small boy, slightly taller than her, with long black hair, staring at her. She stared back, not able to recognize him.

'Who are you?' Mira asked the boy. She did not feel any fear though she seemed somewhat mystified by what was happening.

The boy blinked his eyes once. 'You are Mira,' he said. It wasn't a question.

Mira nodded and said, 'Yes. What's your name?'

'Krishna,' the boy replied.

'Why are you here, Krishna?' Mira asked.

'I don't know,' Krishna replied. 'I was sleeping. I woke up because of all this lightning!'

Mira opened her eyes. She was surrounded by her friends and a couple of teachers. They were all looking at her with strange expressions on their faces.

'Are you alright, Mira?' the class teacher asked, a bit concerned.

Mira nodded, staring blankly at her teacher. What had happened? She was perfectly alright!

'You were sitting like a statue, Mira,' one of her friends remarked. 'Not responding to any of us!'

'You weren't here!' another child remarked, a bit excited. 'You looked like a zombie!'

Swami Nityananda looked at Mira closely. 'Has something like this ever happened before, child?'

Mira shook her head, still trying to figure out what exactly had happened. She remembered the Om chanting and then she remembered seeing a boy. Krishna? But where was he? She looked around but couldn't see him anywhere.

'What happened, Swamiji?' the head mistress later asked Swami Nityananda as she led him out of the assembly hall.

'I think the child went into some kind of a trance,' the Swami replied, thoughtfully. 'Very unusual for such a young child.'

'Nothing to worry about, Swamiji?'

'No, of course not! These things do happen!' the Swami assured her.

≈

Oja stood with Aditi, his woman companion, looking at Mira sleeping on her bed in the earth dimension. Aditi was probing Mira's mind ever so gently, careful not to disturb her or her dreams.

'Is she aware of our presence?' Oja asked quietly.

'Doesn't seem so,' Aditi replied. 'But she's opening rapidly. She went into trance today during the chanting at school!'

'What happened in the trance?'

'Cannot read that, but she was perfectly normal. No fear, no residue.'

'She shouldn't try any more meditation. That will accelerate the whole thing. We are not ready.'

'The Swami's visit was sudden. And we cannot possibly avoid such things!'

'Random events, Oja!'

≈

Once again, Mira became aware of the presence of the two beings across the veil as she slept. She could feel one of them very close to her, almost touching her. She stirred in her sleep and tried to reach out to the presence. As soon as she did that, the presence withdrew.

In the other dimension, across the veil of consciousness, Aditi stepped back, withdrawing her mind from Mira.

'She seems aware of my probing,' she said quietly. 'There was a response.'

'Then let her sleep.' Oja said, looking directly at Aditi.

'Extraordinary!' Aditi whispered. 'She's already sensing across dimensions!'

≈

Mira stood alone on the balcony of her house, overlooking the garden. She was staring silently into space, her mind empty, when she saw a small squirrel scampering up a tree. She smiled and focused on the squirrel. In a few seconds, her whole consciousness seemed to fuse with the squirrel's. She softly called the squirrel to herself. She spoke to it in her head:'Come here, little one, come to me!'

The squirrel turned and seemed to look directly at Mira, its nose twitching in the air.

'Come, come to me,' Mira repeated.

The squirrel took a few tentative steps towards Mira, then stopped, sniffing the air. And then, it darted towards Mira, climbed up the balcony, and came right to her feet, its nose turned up, still twitching.

Mira smiled brightly at the squirrel. 'We're friends now, aren't we?' she asked.

The squirrel twitched its nose. Mira imagined the squirrel agreeing with her.

The Awakening

Kalki was absorbed in deep meditation when she felt a consciousness tugging at her. Her body was jerked out of its trance-like state. She did not open her eyes as she knew that nothing in the physical universe could have pulled her out of meditation. She concentrated inwardly, her consciousness spreading out in ever-widening circles. In a few moments, she could feel Mira in her consciousness, tugging at her, reaching out to her.

Kalki now focused her consciousness on Mira, drawing Mira into her own presence. Mira was physically asleep but her inner being was wide awake.

'Mira,' Kalki whispered softly in Mira's sleep.

Mira stirred, her inner being reaching out and touching Kalki.

'Can you feel me, my child?' Kalki asked.

'Yes,' Mira's inner being replied. A ripple of joy radiated from Mira's inner being and entered Kalki's consciousness.

Kalki smiled. 'You are waking up, my child!'

Mira's sleeping body stirred again. Something deep within her was trying to break out through the dense layers of sleep. Kalki, sensing her struggle, reached out to Mira and a portion of Kalki's being entered Mira's heart, ever so gently—a movement of silence within silence.

Mira, her mind and body still in deep sleep, could only sense the movement—a shaft of white light entering her heart and going straight through, swift and silent—in her dream. She saw a bright light descending from a celestial height into her heart and turning into a blue butterfly, fluttering its glowing wings, scattering speckles of blue and golden light all around her.

Mira smiled in her sleep and her body stirred to wakefulness.

Kalki withdrew her consciousness into her own inmost heart, a heart boundless in expanse, fathomless in depth. Still deeper within her, in those fathomless depths of being, a universe within a universe, Krishna sat still in meditation, his inner gaze now upon a little girl on earth waking up to eternal life, endless existence. As it was always meant to be.

≈

It was the early hours of Mira's eighth birthday. Mira lay still on her bed, wide awake within, completely conscious of her surroundings, as if something or someone in her was seeing without the need for external light. Everything around her seemed bathed in a soft bluish light. Somewhere far in the distance, she could see a pair of eyes looking intently at her—disembodied, glowing like stars in the empty dark. Mira did not feel any fear or nervousness; she felt completely at ease. She stirred gently on her bed, trying to open her physical eyes. But she couldn't. She tried harder, then realized that she couldn't wake herself. She stopped trying and sank back into sleep. *It is a dream*, she thought to herself. But then it immediately struck her that she was conscious of herself sleeping and dreaming. That seemed somewhat strange. *How can I know that I am sleeping and dreaming?* She felt the gaze of those eyes getting more intense. There was love in those eyes, but not the kind of love Mira could understand or respond to. She kept wondering how it was possible to know that one was asleep and dreaming while one was asleep and dreaming.

'It is called a waking sleep, Mira,' a soft voice whispered inside her. 'Your body is asleep, but your mind is completely awake.'

'Is my mind separate from my body then?' Mira whispered back.

'You will soon understand that, my dear,' the voice replied.

'When I grow up?' Mira asked. Her father used to say, 'You will understand when you grow up, Mira.'

'You *are* grown up, Mira!' The voice spoke again, quiet and gentle.

'But I'm just going to be eight!' Mira replied.

'That is how old your body is, Mira. What if you are not just your body?'

'How can that be?'

'Where is your body now, Mira?' the voice asked.

Mira tried to sense her body but, in deep sleep, could not. There seemed to be no body. For a moment, Mira felt confused—a state she had never experienced before—but it passed as quickly as it had come.

'I don't know!' she said quietly.

'You do,' the voice said softly. 'Look again.'

And immediately Mira saw her body sleeping on the bed. She herself was hovering above her own sleeping body. She had never had a dream like this before, she thought. Yet, she felt no fear. That too was quite strange.

'Is that really my body,' she asked, 'or a dream body?'

A force seemed to raise her gently to a higher vantage point from where she could see not only her own body lying on the bed but even her parents sleeping in the room adjoining hers. The house had become transparent, the walls had turned to glass. Before she could grasp what was happening, she could see the entire landscape below her, everything like glass, utterly transparent to her vison.

'This is a very strange dream!' she said to the voice inside her.

'This is not a dream, Mira,' the voice whispered back. 'This too is an experience but different from what you are used to.'

'Who are you?' Mira asked after a while, now curious. 'Can I see you?'

In a trice, Mira was transported across space and time. Ages flashed past in some cosmic memory, and space itself seemed to curve till Mira stood on another ground, breathing another air.

'Mira?'

Mira saw her standing before her, tall, imposing, beautiful. A veil seemed to be lifting from Mira's mind.

'Do you remember?' the woman asked, smiling tenderly.

The veil lifted completely. Mira recognized her—the same eyes brimming with formidable love, the same radiant face, the same overwhelming luminous form she had grown to adore over the years. *She hasn't changed at all*, Mira thought to herself. *Like a goddess*, she remembered.

'Mother?' Mira stepped closer, her eyes looking up into those fathomless eyes that seemed to hold secrets of many lifetimes.

Kalki smiled. 'You remember, my child?'

'Of course, Mother. You have always lived in me. In my deepest dreams!'

'Do you understand now, you're not eight at all.' Kalki asked, gentle as ever.

Mira smiled radiantly. 'But I shall be. Somewhere on earth.'

'Yes, the body.' Kalki's voice trailed off.

'Are you still struggling with the body, Mother?' Mira asked, as some of her ancient memories stirred back into consciousness in her—the old struggles, the long-drawn battles fought deep in the very cells of the body, the anguish of the separation, and the ecstasy of the union in a single frame, almost a single breath, one melting into the other. And then the hordes of the *asuras*, in all shapes and sizes, with their enormous hungry energies, coming in endless waves, one upon the other, each wave threatening to wash out all the work done. The body, as Mira now recalled, was the last refuge of the asura.

'The body still resists,' Kalki said slowly. 'But there is hope now. *You* will take the next step!'

Mira could sense the silent force of Kalki's will in her words—this was much more than hope; it was a command.

'What is the next step, Mother?' Mira asked. 'I do not remember.'

'There is no memory of it, Mira.' Kalki replied. 'The Knowledge does not exist. No one knows how it will happen. Or whether at all it will happen.'

'The asuras?' Mira asked looking straight into Kalki's eyes. 'Are they aware?'

'No,' Kalki said firmly. 'They are not aware at all.'

'So, what happens now, Mother?'

'The Knowledge will grow in you, Mira.'

'In me?' Mira knew what that meant.

'You will have to bear the Knowledge as it grows and keep it safe.'

Mira stood speechless as Kalki's words sank in.

'You will have to be very careful, Mira, as it grows. It must be kept always guarded.' Kalki continued slowly, carefully. 'No one must suspect. The asuras do not know about you—not yet anyway. And Krishna himself veils you. But still, you must be careful.'

'Is Krishna still with you, Mother?' Mira asked.

'He's here,' Kalki said, placing her right palm on her chest. 'Always here.'

'Then what is the fear? Where is the doubt?'

'There is no fear or doubt, Mira. Where Krishna is, fear and doubt cannot be. But the battle is real. The power of the asuras is real.'

'So is Krishna!' Mira said with complete confidence.

Kalki smiled. 'Yes, indeed. So is Krishna.'

'I think he came to me, Mother,' Mira said. 'I had gone into a trance at school.'

'I know. And he is with you. He will prepare you.'

Mira smiled. All the memories were waking up in her, and the veils of time were falling off, one by one. All eternity was opening to her inner seeing.

≈

And Mira woke up on the morning of her eighth birthday, every detail of her dream vivid, alive. She sat up on the bed, stretching her limbs, as the first rays of the sun streamed in through the window of her room. She thought of her mother in the next room. Instantly, she could see her mother's body across the wall. She was still asleep.

'Wake up, Ma,' she willed quietly.

Esha, in her sleep, felt a gentle but firm touch on her skin. She woke up immediately and sat up on her bed. It had felt like Mira's touch. But there was no one in the room.

≈

Kalki smiled to herself. She concentrated for a moment on Krishna and then spoke to him in her heart: 'Krishna! Our Mira is awake!'

And she could sense, deep in her soul, Krishna's divine smile spreading across her being. She knew then that the time had come. She closed her eyes and slowly sank into Krishna's consciousness.

≈

Aditi had kept awake the whole night. Oja had remained in a meditative quietude throughout. They knew that it was the eve of Mira's eighth birthday. The decisive night before she would awake.

And at the very moment Mira awoke on her bed across the veil of consciousness, Aditi and Oja both became fully alert, their gaze resting on Mira, trying to fathom her mind as she awoke. Both saw the bluish light which bathed Mira's body and mind. Both realized simultaneously that Krishna had taken direct charge. The awakening was now imminent.

And then they saw Mira wake her mother by an effortless mental command. They knew then that Mira was awake. The eighth birthday, as was predicted of old.

Vajrada the Asura

Two men huddled around a fire in a forest clearing, sharing a hookah. The fire was burning steady and strong in the cold, windless night.

'You wished to speak to me, Vajrada?' The younger of the two spoke first, passing the hookah to the elder.

Vajrada pulled the hookah closer and inhaled. The water in the hookah gurgled audibly. 'I can sense Kalki's presence growing stronger, Tarak.'

'You still hold on to that Kalki legend, Vajra!' Tarak said in a slightly indulgent tone. 'Humans have passed beyond devas and avatars!'

Vajra exhaled slowly, watching the smoke from his lips spiral into the air. 'Humans are not my concern. Nor the devas, for that matter. It is earth that I'm concerned about.'

Vajra passed the hookah to Tarak.

'What about earth?' Tarak asked, drawing the hookah to his lips.

'The occultists are speaking of a new species....'

'A new species? On earth?'

'Yes, Tarak.'

'What kind of species, Vajra?'

'Not too sure of the details, but certainly not like the humans...'

Tarak turned to look closely at Vajrada, clearly intrigued. He himself had neither interest in nor access to the occultists. Most amongst his tribe regarded the occultists as outliers—mysterious and foreboding. Vajrada was one of the few who could access the occultists.

'Like the devas, then?'

'Yes, superior to humans, it seems. That is what I could gather.' Vajrada said pensively.

'Like the *Übermensch* of the German visionary?'

Vajrada looked at Tarak. The German visionary was a prophet of sorts among the asuras. 'Übermensch? The highest form of Man, the consummation of the human species.'

Tarak took a long pull at the hookah. 'Something like the devas! Well, that does not sound good! But what's the connection with Kalki?'

'Kalki is not a myth, Tarak—an avatar who will come riding a white horse to destroy evil on earth and will usher in the age of the gods! Kalki is the one who will give birth to the new species. And the new species will be beyond our reach.'

Tarak was taken aback by the revelation. He stared speechlessly into the fire and Vajrada continued smoking the hookah.

'Is this what the occultists are saying?' Tarak asked after a long pause.

'Yes, but it's all very much shrouded in mystery.'

'Have you probed the yogis?'

'The yogis have no such knowledge.'

'Then how do the occultists know?'

'That is why they are occultists, Tarak—they have occult knowledge.'

Tarak pulled the hookah closer. 'And you are sensing Kalki's presence?'

Vajrada nodded, lost in thought.

'Care to explain?'

'Explain what?'

'What exactly are you sensing? How do you know it is Kalki?'

'All very indeterminate,' Vajrada said slowly. 'I have always sensed Kalki's presence since she has been on earth. You know that!'

Tarak, and the rest of the asuras, knew that Vajrada was aware of Kalki's presence on earth. None of the asuras believed that of course, but none dared to question Vajrada. Not only was Vajrada one of the oldest of the tribe of asuras, but the most advanced in yogic power and consciousness. He could sense things that were beyond the ken of most asuras. He was the only one among the asuras who had any inkling of the overmind. To the rest, the overmind was purely mythological—the abode of the ancient devas, beings of divine radiance and knowledge.

'You sense Kalki as feminine, Vajrada? Isn't Kalki supposed to be an avatar of Vishnu?'

Vajrada kept quiet for a while. It was true that he had always felt Kalki's presence as overwhelmingly feminine. No one amongst the asuras quite believed him for it was common belief that Kalki would be Vishnu's avatar, therefore, male. How could Vishnu take a feminine incarnation? Yet, Vajrada knew in his bones that Kalki was feminine. But did it really matter? Masculine or feminine, Kalki would spell the end of their reign.

'Yes,' he said finally to Tarak. 'Kalki is feminine—this I have always felt and known. But she as the first of a new species…?' His voice trailed off.

They continued smoking the hookah as the night turned colder and darker.

≈

Datta was the chief amongst the occultists. An accomplished Tantric with extraordinary yogic attainments. It was believed among the occultists that Datta was the only living occultist who had access to the overmind, the plane of the great gods. No one, of course, knew whether he actually ever used that access. But Datta was equally revered and feared among the occultists and the asuras alike.

Datta was sitting outside in his sprawling garden when he was approached by Vajrada in the subtle plane. 'Am I intruding, Datta?'

Vajrada, being the eldest of the asuras, was himself a much-revered being, even among the devas. He was perhaps one of the very few who had direct access to Datta and could regard Datta as almost an equal.

'No, Vajra,' Datta responded. 'You're welcome.'

'I can sense Kalki's presence and power growing, Datta.' Vajrada said solemnly.

Datta nodded. 'So can we, Vajra. She would be more than three hundred in human years now.'

'But she is not an immortal, in spite of all her yoga!' Vajrada said with some force.

'But, Vajra, she has Vishnu with her. Doesn't that change the equation?'

'But Vishnu is with some of us too, Datta.'

Datta smiled knowingly. He knew that Vajra had once been in almost constant inner touch with Vishnu. But that was ages ago. 'Vajra, all I know is that Kalki shares something personal with Vishnu.'

'So, does that mean she will *become* an immortal?'

'*Become*?' Datta asked, somewhat amused. 'How is that possible?'

'By yoga, you know. And if Vishnu wills it.'

'Vishnu will not will any such thing. The laws of death are immutable. Even the avatars have to consent to death. You know that, Vajra, even Vishnu had to die. And not once!'

'And yoga?' Vajrada persisted.

'There is no such yoga either, Vajra. The atman is immortal, that the yogis know. But the immortality of the body is quite another matter.'

'So, will Kalki succumb to physical death? Three hundred years is quite beyond yogic limits!'

Datta smiled again. 'Frankly, I do not know, Vajra, our knowledge does not go that far. Kalki is not an ordinary human yogini—she is an avatar.'

'How much do you know of the new species, Datta?'

Datta looked hard at Vajrada. 'Next to nothing.'

'You would have some indication? From your overmind contact?'

'Overmind contact?' Datta chuckled softly. 'Whoever told you about that?'

'We hear things, Datta. We are the asuras, after all!'

'There is no such contact, Vajra. Sometimes some form of occult intuitive knowledge comes through. And I'm not always sure of the origin of such intuitions.'

'Not even you, Datta?'

Datta smiled self-deprecatingly. 'I don't think anyone can possess infallible knowledge of all things.'

'But the knowledge of the new species is one of those things that has come to you, Datta?'

'I wouldn't call it knowledge, Vajrada. Maybe an indication, an intuition.'

'This is a matter of crucial importance to us, Datta, and you should know that!'

'What is of crucial importance, Vajra?'

'The possibility of a new species on earth—it will change the game. And the rules!'

Datta went into deep meditation. Vajrada waited patiently.

It was after a long while that Datta opened his eyes again and looked directly at Vajrada. 'What is it that you wish to know, Vajra?'

'Is a new species on earth a possibility now?'

'Yes,' Datta said, nodding very slowly, as if drawing the knowledge out of some fathomless depth.

'And this species will be like the present humans?' Vajrada asked.

'Like the present humans?' Datta repeated slowly, deliberately. 'I don't know. I don't see anything like that.'

'What do you see, Datta?'

'A superior form…unlike the human…luminous, tall… like the devas…powerful…'

'Spiritually superior?'

Again, Datta went into silence. Vajrada waited.

'Something else altogether…' Datta spoke after another long pause. 'More than spiritual…a luminous consciousness…' Datta's voice faded into silence.

Vajrada bowed and withdrew from Datta's consciousness. He had learned something significant.

The Twelfth Year

Kalki, quite frail and exhausted, sat in meditation, invoking Krishna. It was past the midnight hour. In just a few hours, Mira would be waking up to her twelfth birthday.

Soon she felt a gentle, soothing vibration in her depths and her whole being trembled in divine delight. 'Krishna!' She whispered his name like a sacred mantra.

'Kalki, I'm here, with you.'

'Today, she will be twelve.'

'Is it done?' Krishna asked.

'Yes, my Lord. All my consciousness is now in her, to the very cells of her body.'

There was deep silence. Time itself seemed to stand still.

'So, the time has come,' Krishna's tone was grave, solemn.

'Yes, Krishna,' Kalki replied. 'She is ready.'

'The memories?'

'It's all there in her psychic.'

'Any resistance?'

'None, Krishna. Her whole being is so beautiful, so surrendered.'

'Because it is *your* consciousness in her body, in every part of her being.'

Kalki remembered all—the dream of the ages, the hope and the prayer of the gods, the incredible labour of love, the incessant struggle and the unbearable weight of the centuries, and the lone love of Krishna, in every vibration of her being, in every cell of her body, bearing her across the threshold of inevitable death to that destined birth which would change time and human fate.

An immense wave of gratitude rose up from her heart.

'I am ready to let go of this body, Krishna, once the transference is complete.'

Krishna was aware. And once the transference was complete, Kalki's old body would no longer be needed. The work would continue unbroken in Mira's body. But this was knowledge no one else would possess but he, in his infinite knowing, and Kalki, in the depths of her soul, till the destined hour.

'Are the guardians aware of the transference?' Krishna asked.

'No, I have veiled that knowledge from them. Do you want them to know?'

'Not yet,' Krishna said. 'What about the occultists?'

'The occultists are beginning to sense the coming, but they are still probing.'

'And the asuras?'

'Only the eldest. He is in touch with the occultists.'

'What does he know?'

'That there will be a new species, a new birth.'

'How did he get it?'

'From the occultist.'

'But the occultists don't know the details, do they?'

'They don't. The knowledge is safe.'

'Once they understand, they will get desperate.'

'I'm aware, Krishna. And as my presence and power grow in her, she will draw their attention.'

'This time, you cannot be veiled, Kalki. The battle will be out in the open.'

'Will you not intervene this time, Krishna?'

As soon as Kalki asked the question, she understood.

Mira herself was the intervention.

Exactly as planned.

That brought a smile to her face.

≈

Oja and Aditi, the guardians, were watching over Mira as she slept on her bed across the veil of consciousness. In another hour it would be the dawn of Mira's twelfth year, and both knew what that meant.

'It is the fifth hour after midnight for her. She wakes in an hour or so.'

'Twelve years,' Aditi said in a hushed tone. 'This year she discovers who she is.'

'As foretold,' Oja said, solemnly.

'Will that knowledge ever be given to us, Oja,' Aditi asked quietly.

'No, Aditi,' Oja replied. 'We are her guardians only. The knowledge of who she is will make it more difficult for us to do our work.'

'Yes, I'm aware, Oja.'

Oja smiled. 'Is there a need in you to know?'

Aditi turned to face Oja. 'Yes.'

'Why?'

'I have an intuition.'

'Keep it at that, you don't need to know anything.'

'The asuras?'

'Yes, they are cunning little devils!'

'I'm aware, Oja. But where does my intuition come from?'

'From Mira herself. When you probe her mind.'

'Yes, of course.'

Aditi felt Mira stir in her sleep. She immediately became alert. Oja too turned his focus on the sleeping Mira.

'She stirs,' Aditi said.

'Something is moving her, it seems.'

Aditi probed gently into Mira's mind but could not—she felt a luminous veil over her that she could not penetrate. She realized immediately what was happening.

'Oja, she is veiled from me.'

Oja turned his attention to Mira. He too felt the luminous veil over her.

'Our work is done,' Oja declared. 'She doesn't need our protection anymore.'

'Yes, Oja, I realize that. The Mother herself veils her now.'

Oja and Aditi faded completely from Mira's awareness.

≈

Mira was waking up. She was aware of the two beings watching over her. She now knew that these were protective beings, emanations of the Mother. When she felt Aditi probing her mind, she gently drew a veil over herself. She then felt Oja's attention on her. And then, almost immediately, both withdrew from her consciousness. Mira knew instinctively that no outer protection was any longer needed—she could now feel the Mother within her, a loving and radiant presence in her inmost heart.

And as soon as she thought of the Mother, she was with her, in her living presence.

'Mother!' Mira reached out to her in her consciousness and touched her glowing presence.

Kalki lifted Mira up in her being. It felt like being lifted onto a velvety cloud of liquid light.

'A very happy birthday to you, my child.'

Mira smiled and sank deeper into the liquid light.

'My twelfth year!' she said to Kalki.

'A decisive year, my child,' Kalki whispered. 'From now on, you and I will be together all the time. I will live in you, think and know in you, will and act in you—one with you in all things and beings. Are you ready, my child?'

Mira breathed deep and slow, absorbing the cloud of liquid light into the very substance of her being. 'Yes, Mother,' she whispered. 'I am, because you are with me.'

'Then, as your mother, I command—awake!'

And Mira's consciousness immediately lit up from within, and a bright golden light poured out of her and spread like lightning waves across all space, lighting up even the darkest recesses of being.

Mira woke up in that golden radiance, and all the knowledge of men and gods, living, dead and unborn, came flooding into her yearning spirit. Time, past, present and future, coalesced into a single inner knowing. Mira knew, at that instant, who she was, and what she was meant to become.

The Realization

In her cave of tapasya—a quiet room in an isolated house somewhere in the Himalayas—veiled by Krishna himself from all inner and outer gaze and knowledge, Kalki let out a long breath, and invoking Krishna in her soul, withdrew her prana from the body. The body, letting go of the sacred prana with gratitude and bliss, went into deep sleep, never to wake again.

As the old body died, Kalki awoke to full consciousness in the body of the twelve-year-old Mira. It was like waking from a dream, seamless and fluid. One moment she was in her old, exhausted body that had been hers for over three centuries, and almost the very same moment, she was in a new body that she had herself formed out of her *tapas teja*—her force of spiritual askesis. She smiled inwardly to herself. The work was done, the axis of earth's being had tilted away from night, towards eternal Day.

She who was Mira in the child's body dissolved joyously into Kalki in the psychic, and Mira and Kalki became one—as they always were. Kalki, the luminous incarnation of Vishnu's consciousness, was now Mira, the culmination of a million years of earth's evolution from dumb matter to complete self-consciousness. A wave of bliss spread slowly, in ever-widening circles, across all conscious life, and the whole universe was electrified for a brief instant in time, and in that moment, time itself was transformed.

≈

Across a distance not measurable in space or time, in a subtle and rarefied plane of Overmental consciousness—orders higher than the human and the asuric—the great devas, immortal and radiant in their beings, felt the cosmic shockwaves of the event. Ganesha, in his cosmic consciousness spanning all space and time, knew immediately what had happened.

He turned inward and smiled. It was done, the event that would begin the new age, awaited by the gods since humanity took its first infant steps towards consciousness. He could still see, in that prodigious cosmic memory of his, with infallible clarity, how the first primate looked up at the ancient skies of earth, wondering what it was all about. It wasn't thought yet but something that would, rapidly and surely, evolve into thought and imagination, something like a cerebral spark, a flicker of mind, leaping out of unconscious matter into the vastness of space.

He felt a surge of divine bliss. The first conquest, the decisive and irreversible tilting of the scales. As he happily contemplated the singular significance of the event, he felt Lakshmi approaching him. He turned towards Lakshmi as she came to Ganesha and stood before him, a smile playing about her lips. She too had felt the event.

'Kalki's work is done on earth,' she said. 'Victory to Krishna!'

'She let go of her old body,' Ganesha said slowly. 'And awoke in another, without break in time or consciousness. That is a decisive victory!'

Lakshmi, in her inner vision, could see the divine event unfold. 'A cosmic step forward for humanity! But are they ready?'

Narad strolled in, pensive, with a sparkle in his eyes. 'They are not, Lakshmi,' he said. 'The transformation of humanity is a long way off. Kalki's work on earth will not be known to many—perhaps only to the yogis and the seers. And there aren't too many of them around anyway!'

Ganesha nodded, instantly understanding Narad's drift. 'The ever-cynical Narad!'

'Nay, not cynical, Ganesha, but realistic. I am the eternal realist and you gods are the eternal idealists.'

'But without our idealism, dear Narad, earth would've gone to the asuras long ago! *They* are the true realists, not you.'

Ganesh smiled again. 'Lakshmi is correct, O Muni! The idealism of the devas is a force in evolution, not a mere belief or attitude!'

Narad bowed, smiling back. 'I accept, O Ganesha. But you will agree with me that Kalki's attainment will be of little value to present humanity. By the time the common man begins to understand her work on earth, it may be too late!'

'Kalki's conquest is not for present humanity, O Narad!' Ganesha declared quietly.

'That has come to my knowledge, Ganesh. Kalki is the prototype of a new species and not the destroyer of the old. Once she accomplishes her work on earth, the old will become redundant and irrelevant.'

'What will happen to the old? The present human?' Lakshmi asked, looking at Ganesha.

Ganesha looked inward for a moment before responding to Lakshmi. 'They will continue to exist on earth with the new species just as the apes continue to exist today along with the humans.'

'And the present humans will be to the new species what the apes are to the present humans?' Narad asked rhetorically and then added, 'Hopefully not!'

'But seriously,' Lakshmi asked again, 'do the present humans have no hope of benefiting from Kalki's work?'

'If they can free themselves from their asuric obsessions, maybe!' Ganesha said to Lakshmi. 'But Kalki's battle is for a change of consciousness now, not in some distant future, and *that* is not very likely to happen soon.'

'I have seen into the future of humanity, Lakshmi,' Narad said solemnly. 'Which makes me cynical, as Ganesha claims I am. I have seen humans grow greedier, crueller, and increasingly self-destructive. This does not bode well for the human future!'

'But Kalki's work,' Lakshmi said, 'is it not for humanity? Is that not Krishna's eternal promise—*yada yada hi dharmasya, glanir bhavati bharata?*'

'Vishnu's will is for the truth-consciousness to manifest upon earth, Lakshmi. And *that* is Kalki's battle. She does not fight against evil, as most on earth believe, but she fights against the resistance of unconsciousness, of tamas, so that Truth may manifest. And whenever and wherever Truth manifests, the evil disappears of itself. No one has to fight it. And that is Kalki's whole plan—Mira will bring in the age of truth-consciousness, and the work will be done!'

'Yes, I have seen that in my deepest visions,' said Narad. 'Mira is the living consciousness of Truth—what she brings to earth is not just truth-consciousness but a species that will embody and manifest this consciousness. The next evolution!'

'And Kalki dying to herself in one body and simultaneously awaking in another is the key event,' Ganesha added. 'It is the first step life on earth takes towards immortality.'

'Mind you, Kalki still had to abandon the old body,' Narad pointed out gently. 'That's not really immortality.'

'Trust you to pick the nitty-gritty, Narad.' Ganesha said. 'The transition from the old to the new body was seamless, unbroken in consciousness. Please consider that. And, more significantly, Kalki prepared Mira's body and consciousness out of her own being and consciousness, *before transiting*. And not only that—Kalki prepared Mira through several lifetimes for this event. Now, if that is not Krishna's miracle, what is?'

Narad considered Ganesha's words for a moment and broke into a smile. 'Narayan! Narayan!' Chanting sonorously, he walked away.

'This is indeed a step towards physical immortality,' Lakshmi said quietly. 'The long promised *amritam* for humanity. Except that humanity will not reap the fruits of the long labour of the ages.'

'But, Lakshmi, the new species will not fall from the sky. It will be born out of humanity. Think of present humanity as the caterpillar, the new species as the butterfly, and Mira as the chrysalis.'

'Ah, that is beautiful, Ganesha!' Lakshmi beamed. 'And when the butterfly emerges, all the evil and violence will be a distant memory of a bygone stage.'

'Maybe even the memory will not be needed. It will be a new race, a new species.'

Lakshmi nodded. 'May Krishna's will be done! May Kalki's work be accomplished! May Mira manifest! Om!'

'Om!' Ganesha repeated, closing his eyes.

≈

Datta was jerked out of his meditation when the shockwaves hit him. The occult knowledge of what had happened flooded into his inner mind. *One being on earth had conquered death physically.* He opened his eyes and looked up into the sky. A single streak of lightning flashed across the clear morning sky. This was a sign of the gods, and Datta, the eldest of the occultists, understood. An age had just ended, and another begun, precipitated by one single event, an event seeded into the fabric of the universe at the very beginning of time.

Datta silently bowed to the supreme godhead of which he himself was an emanation. He felt Vishnu, deep in his heart, acknowledge his obeisance.

'Datta,' he heard a small voice inside him.

He turned his attention to the voice. It was Tara, his consort.

'Yes, Tara?' He asked.

'The Asura wants your time.'

Datta knew Tara was referring to Vajrada. 'Let him come.'

In a moment, Vajrada was in his presence, bathed in his dull yellow aura.

'Yes, Vajra, what brings you here?' Datta asked, though he knew perfectly well what had brought Vajrada to him.

'It's about Kalki.'

'Yes, I am aware,' Datta said. 'What about her, Vajra?'

'Her presence has suddenly grown overwhelming. I was waiting for her passing but something else seems to have happened. There was a cosmic event this morning!'

'The birth of Kalki, as foretold,' Datta's tone was solemn. 'The beginning of a new age.'

'But Kalki was already on earth, growing old. How can there be a new birth?'

'Well, not exactly a birth, a transference, shall we say?'

'I do not understand,' Vajrada said.

'Kalki gave up her old body this morning and entered a new one!'

'On the same day? But that's not possible!'

'But it has happened as I say, Vajra.'

'Where is the new body?' Vajrada asked with keen interest. 'Where has Kalki taken birth?'

'No, not taken birth exactly—entered a new body.'

'A body that was already there? She has taken possession?'

Datta smiled. 'No, not a possession. I frankly do not know how to explain.'

'Please, tell me the way it is, the way it happened.'

'Let me try—she gave up her old body and woke up in this new body.'

'Woke up? Just like that?' Vajrada sounded sceptical. 'And this body was just waiting…to be…er…possessed?'

'No, Vajra. To understand this, you will have to possess a psychic consciousness, which you don't. A human being can unite consciously with a divine being in his or her psychic and become one with it.'

Vajrada tried his best to comprehend. Datta looked at him with great compassion. If asuras possessed the possibility of psychic consciousness, they wouldn't be asuras at all.

'Not getting it,' Vajrada said finally. 'But pray tell me, where is Kalki now, in whose body, where?'

'Vajra, I do not know. That knowledge is hidden from all.'

'Even from you, great Datta?'

Datta smiled at Vajrada. 'Yes, even from me.'

'But how was this done? Such a thing has never occurred—an instantaneous transition from one body to another, without actually dying?'

'Kalki would have mastered the processes of prakriti. It involves occult knowledge beyond my understanding.'

'So, what does this imply for the future of humanity?'

'From all that I can gather, Vajra, it is a divine event, engineered by Vishnu himself. Kalki has become a unique phenomenon—she represents in herself a dying species and a newborn one.' Datta said gravely, understanding the significance of what he was saying. And the one thing Vajrada was dreading to hear. 'She first prolonged her human lifespan to three centuries by her will and tapasya, and then she engineered a simultaneous transition to a new being!'

'Thereby bypassing death!' said Vajrada, equally grave. He was just beginning to understand the gravity of the 'event'. 'So, you were right! A new species will emerge on earth.'

'As superior to present-day humans as humans are to apes,' said Datta, staring into the far distance, looking into the very heart of time.

Datta's words sank deep into Vajrada. 'A spiritually superior species, maybe with direct access to the gods!'

'Maybe more than that, Vajra.'

'More than that?'

'Why not? A species capable of surpassing even the gods!'

The ground seemed to tremble beneath Vajrada. Or so he felt in his consciousness. 'Surpassing the gods? Humans surpassing the gods? That seems impossible!'

'But it will be a new species, Vajra. Not human anymore!'

An old phrase returned to Vajrada's mind. *Übermensch. The highest form of Man.*

'Which will not be Man at all,' Datta completed, reading his thought.

'Nor a deva?'

'Man must be surpassed,' Datta said firmly, 'for Man to be.'

'And if Man is surpassed, will the asuras be far behind?'

'The asuras too, Vajra, the asuras too!'

'What is the future, then, Datta? I feel a deep disquiet in me, I need to know.'

'If Kalki's plan comes to fruition, Vajra,' Datta spoke slowly, weighing his words, 'the asuras will slowly become irrelevant. And so, for that matter, will the devas.'

And what he left unsaid, Vajrada grasped. Even the occultists will become irrelevant.

After a long pause, Datta spoke again—'Isn't that what you asuras fear the most? Irrelevance?'

'Yes, a fate worse than extinction.'

'But what is the purpose of the asura?'

'To become devas, to possess heaven and earth. But you know that, Datta. It has been so from the beginning of time.'

Datta knew that. The earth plane is equally precious to the devas and the asuras for the same reason—earth is the only plane where beings can evolve, become more than what they are. The devas and the asuras, for all their might and pomp, have one final limitation—they can never grow in consciousness. To grow in consciousness, they would have to take human birth, and lose all the pomp, power and knowledge in the process.

'But what is the end of it all? Once you possess heaven and earth?' Datta asked.

'The human and the devas will serve the will of the asuras, and the myth of dharma shall forever be erased from consciousness.'

'And Vishnu will allow that?' asked Datta again.

'Vishnu? But once he has given the power of free will, he cannot intervene. Man is free to choose the daivic or the asuric. Why interfere with that?'

'Indeed, why interfere with that!' Datta was slowly withdrawing, beginning to grasp the significance of Kalki's design. *An asuric creation would be chaos, not cosmos. It is in chaos that the asura thrives, in chaos and noise.* Datta closed his eyes as he withdrew into contemplation. *The primeval struggle of consciousness against tamas, cosmos against chaos, evolution against entropy.*

Perhaps, there was an end in sight. A light in the horizon.

The First Born

Mira stood by the window, looking out at the garden, the silence around her palpable. She saw a bee alight on a bright flower in the garden. And then she realized that the bee was not outside in the garden but inside, in her own consciousness. So was the garden, and all the plants, flowers, insects. It was as if the world had turned outside in. She could sense everything outside within her. *This was interesting*. She concentrated for a few moments and the sense grew more vivid, more real. There was no world outside at all, everything was in her. Mira was the world; Mira was the sky. She drew in her breath and held it within. She remembered everything, everyone. She remembered Kalki, the one she had known and loved through the ages as her spiritual mother, the one she was now becoming within herself. She remembered Mira, the little girl she herself was in this lifetime. She remembered Krishna, the eternally nourishing source of her being, and she remembered Som and Esha, her parents in this life; she even remembered Oja and Aditi, her guardian angels, beings of a subtler dimension. She released her breath slowly and closed her eyes.

One by one, as if in a slow-motion movie, scenes of her past lives floated past the screen of her mind—faces, forms, events, dreams, hopes, aspirations, intense struggles, crushing defeats and soaring victories, loves and friendships, some fleeting and some spanning lifetimes, and her own being running through endless spirals of self-becoming like a silver thread weaving everything and everyone into a single fabric of existence. She knew then, without any doubt, that all existence was one, and all existence was she.

When she opened her eyes, she saw Krishna looking at her with a smile. She remembered him as the young boy she had first seen in her trance years ago. He looked the same.

'Krishna!' She ran into his arms joyously. Krishna held her lovingly in his embrace.

'Mira, how you have grown!' Krishna said, beaming with joy.

'Oh, I'm just turning twelve, Krishna!'

'Happy birthday, dear Mira. Twelve is one of my favourite numbers!'

'You have favourites?'

'Oh, sometimes, when I play with numbers.'

Mira grinned. 'You also play with energies and forces, I know that!'

'Has she told you everything?' Krishna asked with a mischievous smile.

'Oh, almost!' Mira said playfully. 'The rest I will find out on my own!'

'That you will!'

Krishna led Mira by her hand into the garden, and they sat down on the soft grass.

Krishna looked at Mira, still smiling. 'You know who I am?'

'I do, Krishna!' Mira held Krishna's hand in hers. 'Because I know who I am.'

'We have so much work to do, Mira.' Krishna said quietly.

'I know. I'm here to complete Kalki's work. As has been decreed by you.'

'It will be a struggle, Mira, a relentless one. Everything will fight back, men will deny and refuse your light, even the devas will resist. And you will struggle all alone, your only strength and support will be the knowledge of who you are, and why you are here.'

Mira heard Krishna with bowed head, every word sinking deep into her consciousness. And as the words entered her consciousness, she could feel waves of bliss rising in her, and she knew that she would never be alone.

'I know that you will be with me in my heart and my soul,' she whispered into his ear, fortified now by an assurance no force or circumstance in the universe would ever affect.

'May your will and strength become one with mine,' Krishna said, holding Mira's hand in his.

Mira stood up and looked into Krishna's eyes. 'May Your will be done, O Krishna!'

Krishna smiled.

Mira slowly sank to her knees and placed her head on his feet.

Krishna raised her up to him.

'Narayan…Narayan!' chanting softly, Krishna faded from Mira's consciousness, leaving her standing alone, but in bliss, suddenly powerful beyond measure, towering above all the earth, her head among the stars, her eyes opening to a new creation beyond the humans and gods. In the far distance, beyond all human or divine measure, beyond the reach of all embodied consciousness, there stood a solitary figure, resplendent, like a star brighter than a thousand galaxies, a figure none would know, or ever reach. Deep within, where she was Kalki, and she was Krishna, she glimpsed that lone resplendent figure, almost like a shooting star in the dark of night, and she smiled.

She was the first born of a divine race.

To the Mother and Sri Aurobindo

APPENDIX 1

The Devas and the Asuras

The Hindu gods exist at various planes—psychological, terrestrial, spiritual and supramental as emanations, representations and embodiments of higher powers and consciousnesses that are in touch with human life on the terrestrial plane.

To grasp the entire significance of this, we will first need to understand the inner, or mystical, structure of the universe we live in. The universe has an external form or structure observable through electromagnetic radiation across the entire spectrum, from radio waves to gamma rays, and an inner form or structure knowable only in consciousness. The external universe is what physics and astrophysics study, and the inner universe is what the mystics experience.

This should not be too difficult to accept. We ourselves have an outer form—the physical, or corporeal, body—that is visible within certain ranges of the electromagnetic spectrum, and an inner form—known to mystics as the subtle body—which, though invisible along the electromagnetic spectrum, is knowable and tangible in our consciousness. Our consciousness, in fact, is the bridge between the outer visible and the inner invisible, extending indefinitely on both ends, for without consciousness extending indefinitely into the outer, the universe wouldn't be visible or knowable at all; and without it extending within, there would be no self-conscious life.

Just as large numbers of nebulae, galaxies, stars and planets exist in the outer visible universe, and at different, higher or lower, orders of complexity and differentiation, so too there are several planes of consciousness within the inner consciousness-universe inhabited by subtle lifeforms ranging from the *daivic*—from the Sanskrit *deva*, meaning divine or radiant—to the *rakshasic*—from the Sanskrit *rakshas*, meaning demon, or demonic. These lifeforms are not figments of imagination but actual living forms beyond the range of the electromagnetic spectrum and therefore invisible to the physical eyes. Reflect on the fact that science does not reject the possibility of ranges beyond the electromagnetic spectrum in the universe. We do not yet know enough to dismiss the possibility of other spectra along which the universe might reveal itself.

Ancient yogic sciences, however, went much farther in their explorations than the empirical or the theoretical sciences of today. The seers of old, the *maharshis*, those original scientists and technologists of consciousness, pushing far beyond the visible and tangible frontiers of our known universe, had accessed ranges of consciousness and existence that would seem sheer magic to the modern scientist. Recall here the two famous adages of the visionary science fiction writer, Arthur C. Clarke: One, *the only way of discovering the limits of the possible is to venture a little way past them into the impossible*; and two, *any sufficiently advanced technology is indistinguishable from magic*. To fully appreciate the import of these thoughts, we need to bear in mind that the most advanced technologies of the future may well be technologies of consciousness.

The devas and asuras in this story are, therefore, neither imaginations of some ancient seer nor are they transmitted cultural constructs—they are real living beings but non-biological and non-temporal; many claim that they are non-material as well, but that is not entirely true: they are material but their materiality is so subtle that they appear invisible or non-material to human perception. However, when these devas and asuras *want* to be seen or felt materially, they can change the density of their matter by the power of their consciousness. We must remember that these asuras and devas are enormously powerful beings, several orders higher than humans in the hierarchy of consciousness.

The devas, as well as the asuras, are in touch with the terrestrial plane and intervene—or interfere, as the case may be—in human affairs whenever necessary. They can be invoked, and their conscious action made manifest in our lives and consciousnesses. It might be easy to think of them as omnipotent or omniscient beings, but they are not. They may be very powerful compared to humans, but they are not omnipotent; they may possess infinite knowledge compared to humans, but they are not omniscient. They are God-like beings, good or evil, living on a particular plane of the consciousness hierarchy, just as we humans do on our terrestrial plane in the same consciousness hierarchy. There are planes and levels below the gods, the human being one of them, and there are planes and levels above the gods.

APPENDIX 2

The Shanti Sloka

Om Purnamadah Purnamidam

This hymn is found in the *Ishavasya Upanishad*, a brief poem of 17–18 verses, one of the shortest of the Upanishads, a philosophical text about the nature of the soul.

ॐ पूर्णमदः पूर्णमिदम् पूर्णात् पूर्णमुदच्यते ।
पूर्णस्य पूर्णमादाय पूर्णमेवावशिष्यते ॥
ॐ शान्तिः शान्तिः शान्तिः ॥

Om pūrṇamadaḥ pūrṇamidam pūrṇāt pūrṇamudacyate.
Pūrṇasya pūrṇamādāya pūrṇamevāvaśiṣyate.
Oṃ śāntiḥ śāntiḥ śāntiḥ.

That is Whole and this is Whole, the perfect has come out of the perfect; having taken the perfect from the perfect, only the perfect remains. Let there be Peace, Peace, Peace.

APPENDIX 3

The Complete Nirvana Shatakam

मनो बुद्ध्यहंकारचित्तानि नाहम्
न च श्रोत्र जिह्वे न च घ्राण नेत्रे
न च व्योम भूमिर् न तेजो न वायु:
चिदानन्द रूप: शिवोऽहम् शिवोऽहम् ॥1॥

mano buddhi ahankara chittani naaham
na cha shrotra jihve na cha ghraana netre
na cha vyoma bhumir na tejo na vaayuhu
chidananda rupah shivo'ham shivo'ham

Neither mind, nor intellect, nor thought nor ego am I
Neither the senses nor ether, earth, fire or air am I,
I am the Self of Eternal Bliss, Shiva am I, Shiva am I.

न च प्राण संज्ञो न वै पञ्चवायु:
न वा सप्तधातुर् न वा पञ्चकोश:
न वाक्पाणिपादौ न चोपस्थपायू
चिदानन्द रूप: शिवोऽहम् शिवोऽहम् ॥2॥

na cha prana sangyo na vai pancha vayuhu
na va sapta dhatur na va pancha koshah
na vak pani-padau na chopastha payu
chidananda rupah shivo'ham shivo'ham

Neither life nor its vital forces am I,
I am beyond the body and its life,
I am neither the elements that make the body,
Nor the gross or subtle sheaths that clothe the soul,
I am beyond all activity, beyond the organs of action,
I am the Self of Eternal Bliss, Shiva am I, Shiva am I.

न मे द्वेष रागौ न मे लोभ मोहौ
मदो नैव मे नैव मात्सर्य भाव:
न धर्मो न चार्थो न कामो ना मोक्ष:
चिदानन्द रूप: शिवोऽहम् शिवोऽहम् ॥3॥

na me dvesha ragau na me lobha mohau
na me vai mado naiva matsarya bhavaha
na dharmo na chartho na kamo na mokshaha
chidananda rupah shivo'ham shivo'ham

I have neither aversion nor desire, neither greed nor delusion;
No envy, arrogance or pride have I,
I am beyond the principles of life and the laws of the world,
I have no desire for wealth, nor even for liberation,
I am the Self of Eternal Bliss, Shiva am I, Shiva am I.

न पुण्यं न पापं न सौख्यं न दु:खम्
न मन्त्रो न तीर्थं न वेदा: न यज्ञा:
अहं भोजनं नैव भोज्यं न भोक्ता
चिदानन्द रूप: शिवोऽहम् शिवोऽहम् ॥4॥

na punyam na papam na saukhyam na duhkham
na mantro na tirtham na veda na yajnah

aham bhojanam naiva bhojyam na bhokta
chidananda rupah shivo'ham shivo'ham

I am beyond virtue and sin, beyond pleasure and pain,
I have no need of mantra or pilgrimage,
I have no need of scripture or ritual,
I am beyond all experience: neither the object of experience nor the experiencer am I,
I am the Self of Eternal Bliss, Shiva am I, Shiva am I.

न मृत्युर् न शंका न मे जातिभेद:
पिता नैव मे नैव माता न जन्म
न बन्धुर् न मित्रं गुरुर्नैव शिष्य:
चिदानन्द रूप: शिवोऽहम् शिवोऽहम् ॥5॥

na mrtyur na shanka na mejati bhedaha
pita naiva me naiva mataa na janmaha
na bandhur na mitram gurur naiva shishyaha
chidananda rupah shivo'ham shivo'ham

I have no fear of death for beyond death am I;
I am beyond duality and have no caste or creed,
I have neither father, nor mother, for beyond birth am I;
I am friend to none, no relation have I,
I am neither the teacher nor the taught, neither master nor disciple am I,
I am the Self of Eternal Bliss, Shiva am I, Shiva am I.

अहं निर्विकल्पो निराकार रूपो
विभुत्वाच्च सर्वत्र सर्वेन्द्रियाणाम्

न चासंगतं नैव मुक्तिर् न मेय:
चिदानन्द रूप: शिवोऽहम् शिवोऽहम् ॥6॥

aham nirvikalpo nirakara rupo
vibhut vatcha sarvatra sarvendriyanam
na cha sangatham naiva muktir na meyaha
chidananda rupah shivo'ham shivo'ham

The all-pervasive changeless, formless Self am I,
I am the Presence in all that is sensing and sensed,
Always equal, calm and unmoved—
I have neither desire for this world nor for liberation,
I am the measureless, the immanent and transcendent,
I am the Self of Eternal Bliss, Shiva am I, Shiva am I.

A Glossary of Sanskrit Words and Phrases

Adhikara: Moral or spiritual right; authority; the capacity or fitness to undertake something, especially in philosophical or spiritual contexts; the inner qualification and preparedness.

Adhyaropa: Means superimposition and is a fundamental concept in Vedanta. It refers to the mistaken attribution, or superimposition, of characteristics to something that does not inherently possess them. In yoga and Vedanta, this usually refers to the superimposition of the unreal, or asat, on the real, or sat. Sat means absolute reality, truth or existence and is also known as Brahman, the ultimate reality which is pure existence, consciousness and bliss—sat-chit-ananda.

Due to ignorance, or avidya, we mistakenly superimpose the world, body and mind onto Brahman, just as one may mistake a rope for a snake in dim light. This false attribution is called Adhyaropa.

Advaita: Non-dual, not two, oneness. There is only one ultimate reality, Brahman, and everything else is just an appearance or manifestation of it.

Ahambhava: Refers to the sense of I-ness, or the feeling of being a separate self or ego; closely tied to the concept of ahankara or ego but more experiential, a felt presence of 'I am this body, this mind, this identity'. Also, see suddha ahambhava.

Aham brahmasmi: I am Brahman, I (aham) am (asmi) Brahman (that ultimate reality).

Ahankara: I-ness, egoism, the principle that gives rise to the sense of 'I' or individuality; the feeling that I am this body, I am the doer (karta bhava) or I am separate from others.

Ajna-chakra: The sixth primary energy centre in the subtle body, according to yogic and Tantric traditions. It's often referred to as the third eye chakra, associated with intuition, insight and inner wisdom.

Ajo nityah shashvato yam purano, na hanyate hanyamane sharire: The individual consciousness neither takes birth nor dies at any time. It has never been created nor will it ever be created. It is unborn, eternal, indestructible and timeless; it is not destroyed when the material body is destroyed. From the Bhagavad Gita, Chapter 2, Verse 20.

Akasha: Space or sky.

Amritam: Refers to immortality, or the immortal essence of the Self; it also means the nectar of immortality. The immortal essence of the Self. The root words are *a* (not), mrita, dead or death So, amṛtam; not subject to death.

Amritasya putrah: Children of immortality or born of the immortal essence.

Ananda: Absolute or spiritual delight, the bliss of the Spirit.

Anirvachaniya: That which cannot be described or defined, cannot be brought into thought or speech.

Annamaya: The physical, material, literally made of food; From annamaya, Annamaya Purusha, the physical Being.

Ansha: Portion.

Asuddhi: Impurity.

Asura: Opposed to the Light, not divine, mainly demonic, evil, adversary of the truth; a hostile being of the mental world (Sri Aurobindo).

Asuric: Relating to or the nature of the asura.

Atma sanstham manah kṛitva na kinchid api chintayet: Having fixed the mind on the Self (atma), one should not think of anything at all. From the Bhagavad Gita, Chapter 6, Verse 25.

Atman: The inmost Self; essence of being, inmost Reality; often understood as the soul in English but more nuanced than the generally accepted meaning of this word. In Vedanta, the atman is the eternal, unchanging, witness-consciousness within all beings; not the body, not the mind, not thoughts or emotions but the seer of all of these.

Avatar: Divine incarnation.

Avidya: Spiritual or fundamental ignorance lack of the knowledge of spiritual truth.

Avyakta: Unmanifest, invisible, unexpressed or formless.

Ayam atma brahman: This Self (ayam atma) is Brahman, absolute and ultimate truth.

Ayushman bhava: May you live long; may you be blessed with a long life.

Bhedbhav: Bheda means difference, division or separation and bhava means feeling, attitude, state of mind or being, so, the feeling or perception of difference or duality.

Bindu: Point; the point of origin, the primordial dot from which all forms emerge; represents Shiva-Shakti in union, undivided, silent, pure potential.

Brahmagati: The path to Brahman or movement (gati) towards Brahman; the attainment of Brahman, or abidance, in the Supreme Reality.

Brahman: the Supreme Reality that is one and indivisible and infinite, besides which nothing else really exists.

Brahmic: Relating to Brahman.

Brahmin: Traditionally, one who belongs to the caste of priests, teachers, scholars, guardians of sacred knowledge; yogically, knower of Brahman, the ultimate reality.

Buddhi: The reason, intelligence, mental power of understanding.

Chaitya purusha: The psychic being; the one who is conscious within.

Chidakasha: Chit is consciousness, awareness, pure knowing and akasha is space, sky, ether, the subtlest of elements; so, the space of consciousness or the inner sky of awareness.

Chit: Pure consciousness; self-awareness of the Absolute.

Chitshakti: Consciousness-force.

Chitta: The basic stuff of mental consciousness.

Chitta vritti: Movements, modifications or fluctuations of the mind; the movements or patterns within the mind-field.

Daivic: Of the devas, divine beings.

Deva: Literally, beings of the Light, bright or radiant ones.

Devi: Goddess; the Divine Shakti; feminine of deva.

Dharma: Action governed by the essential law of one's nature; right moral law; law of the Truth; the cosmic principle.

Dharma yuddha: Battle for dharma, for the right and the true.

Dhyana: Meditation or concentration.

Dhyanam kutra asti, vatsa: Where is your attention or consciousness, child?

Ekam sat: One Truth, One Reality.

Gati: Movement.

Guna: Any one of the three essential modes of energy, sattva, rajas, tamas, of the three primal qualities that form the nature of things.

Guru: Master, teacher, spiritual guide or preceptor.

Gurudev: Term of respect for the Guru; guru, teacher and Deva, lord.

Hookah: Also known as shisha, waterpipe or narghile, it is a traditional device used for smoking flavoured tobacco by passing it through water before inhalation

Hridaye guhayam: Cave of the heart; refers to the innermost sanctum of being, a sacred inner space where the Self or Brahman resides. Hriday is heart, inmost centre of the being, and guha is cave.

Ishvara: Fom *Ish*, to rule, to have power, to master, Ishvara means the Lord, Supreme Controller, Sovereign Self. It denotes one who has complete mastery over creation, time, nature and even Himself.

Jada: Inert, unconscious, lifeless, insentient; in essence, anything that does not have consciousness

Jagat: World, universe, literally, the moving.

Jnana: Wisdom, knowledge; knowledge of Truth.

Jnana yogi: Knower of Truth, one who possesses the highest spiritual wisdom; one who follows the path of Self-knowledge, the path of deep inquiry into 'Who am I?' to realize the true Self (atman), and merge with the Absolute, Brahman.

Kaliyug: Kali refers to the spirit of discord, strife, decay and yug or Yuga refers to age, epoch or cycle. So, kali yug implies the age of spiritual decline and confusion. However, this is a transitional understanding, and there are several layers of mystical and mythical meaning in this phrase.

Kalki: Traditionally, Kalki is the mysterious and powerful tenth avatar of Lord Vishnu, yet to appear, the avatar of the future, the one prophesied to come at the end of Kali Yuga, to restore dharma, righteousness and reset the cosmic cycle.

Karma: Action entailing its consequences.

Karma yoga: The path of spiritual union with the Divine through action, works, a spiritual path where desireless and selfless work (nishkarma karma) becomes a means to liberation.

Karma yogi: One who walks the path of spiritual realization through selfless, devoted, conscious action, action undertaken without attachment to results.

Lobha: Greed, from the root lubh, to desire, to crave. Considered one of the six psychological impurities—*kama* or lust, excessive desire, *krodha* or anger, *moha* or delusion, *mada* or pride and *matsarya* or envy—that prevent liberation.

Loka: World, realm or plane of existence. It refers to different dimensions or levels of consciousness, both material and spiritual, where beings exist based on their evolution.

Mahadeva: Literally, the Great God, traditionally refers to Shiva.

Mahakala: The Great Time or the Supreme Destroyer as Time; traditionally, refers to a fierce aspect of Shiva, the one who dissolves the universe at the end of a cosmic cycle.

Mahamantra: Literally, great mantra.

Maharishi or maharshi: A revered title meaning Great Seer or Sage. It refers to a being of profound spiritual realization, deep wisdom and inner vision, one who has gone beyond the ordinary mind and directly perceived truth or Brahman.

Mahashivratri: Literally, the great night of Shiva, it is a powerful festival dedicated to Lord Shiva, the embodiment of pure consciousness, transformation and inner stillness.

Mahavidyas: Great Knowledge or Great Wisdom symbolized by the ten wisdom goddesses. These goddesses are not just deities to be worshipped but are cosmic forces within consciousness, and tools for transformation.

Mahayogi: A great yogi, one who has realized complete union and identification with the supreme Self, Brahman.

Manas: The sense-mind as opposed to the reason.

Mantra: Set words or sounds having a spiritual significance or power.

Mantra-shastras: Spiritual or yogic study of mantras; the science of mantras.

Maya: The lower Prakriti, as distinguished from the Para Prakriti. Also understood as the cosmic illusion or the veil of appearances that makes the One appear as many, the Eternal seem transient and the Self seem separate. Literally, it means that which measures and limits the Infinite.

Moha: Commonly understood as delusion and attachment arising from delusion, a state of mental confusion where one mistakes the unreal for the real, and clings to what is impermanent.

Moola mantra: Literally, seed mantra.

Muladhara chakra: It is the first of the seven primary energy centres or chakras in the yogic system. It is the root chakra, located at the base of the spine, and is the foundation of our physical and pranic (energetic) being.

Muni: Literally, the silent one, refers to a seer who has turned inward to realize truth through deep meditation, silence and inner wisdom rather than study, scripture or debate.

Namarupa: Literally, name (nama) and form or shape (rupa). Refers to the world of appearances, the dual aspects through which reality manifests and is perceived. Nama refers to the mental concepts, identity, classification, description and character. Rupa refers to the form or the structure perceived by the senses and the mind. Together, namarupa reforest to the entire phenomenal universe.

Narad: A divine sage, devarshi (deva + rishi), and a great devotee of Narayan or Vishnu. Known for his wisdom, devotion, music.

Narayan: The supreme being, the eternal all-pervading consciousness. Literally, the resting or dwelling place of all beings. Krishna or Vishnu are emanations or forms of Narayan.

Neha nanasti kincana: From the *Chandogya Upanishad,* meaning there is none other, there is no second, no duality, no diversity whatsoever. *Neha* means not here (referring to Truth), *nana asti* means there is no other, no duality or multiplicity, *kinchana* means not even a little bit.

Nimitta: Instrument, cause or medium. To realize oneself as a nimitta, or the instrument, of the Divine is the highest realization of the Gita's Karma Yoga.

Nirakara rupo: The form of the formless. This can be understood either as one whose form is formless or one who appears as all forms yet has no form of its own.

Om: The mantra or expressive sound symbol of the Brahman Consciousness.

Om tat sat: Om is the symbol of the absolute being, Brahman, beyond time, form and qualities; *tat* literally means *that*, referring to the Supreme Reality, the Truth, beyond name and form; *sat* means existence, Reality, Truth. Om tat sat is therefore known as the threefold name of Brahman.

Panchakshar mantra: Explained in the story.

Prajna: Higher wisdom, intuitive insight or knowing, pure awareness. It is not just knowledge but the luminous clarity of consciousness itself.

Prakash: Light, luminous clarity, illumination.

Prakriti: Refers to the outer or executive side of the Conscious Force which forms and moves the world. There is the lower or *apara prakriti* and a higher or *para prakriti*.

Prana: Life force, the nervous energy, the vital breath, the half-mental, half-material dynamism which links mind and matter; also, the outgoing breath.

Pranam: Reverent salutation, bowing down or offering respect, usually through a physical gesture like joining hands (namaskar), bowing the head or prostrating fully.

Psychic: All movements and experiences of the soul, those which rise from or directly touch the psychic being.

Psychic being: The soul; when the psyche, a spark of the Divine which is present in all life and matter, begins to develop an individuality in the course of evolution, that psychic individuality is called the psychic being.

Purnata: Completeness, wholeness, perfection.

Rasa: Essence, flavour, juice, emotion or aesthetic experience. It appears in classical Indian art, literature, music, philosophy, Ayurveda and spirituality. It means that which is tasted, not just on the tongue, but by the heart, the mind and the soul.

Raso vai sah, rasam hyevayam labdhvanandi bhavati: From the *Taittirīya Upaniṣhad* (2.7.1). It means that (the Supreme) is Rasa (essence, flavour). Having attained that Rasa, one becomes blissful. This implies that the Divine is not just an abstract concept; it is the essence, the very flavour of existence, the joy behind all joy, the inner juice of life, and having attained that essence, not just intellectually but through direct inner experience, one becomes full of bliss, and the result is ananda, supreme unconditional, spiritual bliss.

Rishi: Seer, sage.

Sadhana: Spiritual practice, self-training and discipline.

Sadhaka: One who practices sadhana, spiritual seeker.

Sadhu: A renunciate, spiritual seeker, holy person in the Indian tradition who has left behind worldly attachments in pursuit of liberation or union with the Divine.

Sadhu-sanskaras: Tendencies to renouncing; subtle impressions of renunciation one carries in one's being.

Sahadharmi: Literally, one who shares the same dharma, a fellow traveller on the path of dharma or spirituality.

Sakshi-bhav: Witness attitude or witness consciousness, the state of detached witnessing.

Samadhi: Traditionally understood as the highest state of consciousness in yoga and meditation, a profound inner stillness where the mind dissolves, and the seeker becomes completely one with the object of meditation or with pure consciousness. However, samadhi can have other meanings and connotations depending upon the yogic context and practice.

Samsara: Traditionally understood as the cycle of birth, death and rebirth, the endless wheel of existence driven by karma and ignorance; also refers to worldly relations, preoccupations and engagements.

Sanatan Dharma: Also known as Hindu dharma, the eternal law and principle of existence, life and society. Sometimes, erroneously, understood to be the Hindu religion. Dharma implies the law or principle that holds, sustains and governs.

Sannyasi: A renunciate, one who has renounced worldly life and personal identity to seek spiritual truth and liberation.

Sanskara: Subtle mental impressions left by thought, action and experience; these impressions form our habits, tendencies and personality.

Sarvam Shiva-mayam: All is filled with Shiva, or everything is permeated by the presence of Shiva; every form, every being, every atom is a manifestation of Shiva.

Sat: Truth, existence or being itself; eternal and unchanging reality.

sat-chit-ananda: An expression that describes the nature of the true Self, atman or Brahman, the Absolute Reality. *Sat* refers to pure Being, eternal and unchanging existence; *chit* refers to pure Consciousness, the all-knowing awareness; *ananda* refers to pure Bliss or divine delight that is part of the triune reality of sat-chit-ananda.

Shakti: Means power, energy or force, specifically, the divine feminine power that creates, sustains and transforms the entire universe. Refers also to the dynamic aspect of the Absolute, the creative energy of Shiva, pure consciousness, and the goddess, the divine mother, the source of all manifestation.

Shishya: Disciple; shishyaa for feminine.

Shiva-vritti: Refers to the inner movement of the mind or consciousness that is turned towards Shiva, or that is in the mode of Shiva. It is a pure, divine mental tendency or state aligned with the qualities of Shiva, the Supreme Consciousness, the witness, the stillness and the detached bliss beyond duality. Also a state where the mind reflects the qualities of Shiva's silence, clarity and non-attachment. In Vedanta, it refers to the movement of the mind that turns inward to realize the non-dual Self.

Shivalinga: The symbol or mark of Shiva, and not a phallic symbol as often misunderstood. It's a cosmic pillar that represents the formless reality of Brahman, the union of Shiva or consciousness and Shakti, force or energy. Some regard it as the very source of creation, sustenance and dissolution.

Shraddha: Means spiritual faith, intuitive knowing or heartfelt conviction. It is a deep inner resonance, a subtle certainty that guides one's mind and heart towards truth, even when one does not have pramana or proof.

Shunyata: Often understood as emptiness, void, but indicates the lack of inherent, independent existence in all phenomena.

Siddhi: Means perfection, attainment or supernatural power, especially because of deep spiritual practice or yogic mastery.

Sthitaprajna: A person of steady wisdom, one whose mind remains calm, balanced and undisturbed no matter what happens in life. This is an important condition of the yoga of the Bhagavad Gita and refers to the sage whose inner awareness is firmly established in the Self or atman.

Sthiti: From the root sthā meaning to stand, or be established, refers to a condition of stability, state, steady condition; also, status.

Suddha ahambhav: See ahambhava; also, the pure sense of I-am without attachment to body, mind or identity; the I that remains when egoism has dissolved.

Suddhi: Purification; yogic purification.

Svayambhu: Explained in the story.

Swarupa: A key idea of Vedanta that means one's true nature, essential form or innate identity, beyond all external appearances, labels or roles. Refers to the eternal, unchanging nature of the Self beyond body, mind, emotions or ego.

Tamas: One of the three gunas, fundamental qualities of nature, described in Sankhya Yoga and the Bhagavad Gita: represents inertia, darkness, ignorance, stagnation and death.

Tantras: A collection of spiritual scriptures and teachings rooted in Hinduism, Buddhism and Jainism, focusing on the direct experience of the divine through rituals, mantras, meditation, yoga, deity worship and often esoteric practices. The literal meaning of Tantra is that which expands and refers to a system to expand consciousness.

Tantric: Related to the Tantra.

Tapas teja: The inner fire or force of austerity, spiritual heat, discipline and refers to inner radiance, brilliance, divine energy and force.

Tapasya: Deep spiritual discipline, austerity or intense inner effort undertaken for the sake of self-purification, transformation and realization of Truth.

Tat twam asi: That, ultimate reality, the Self, you are. *Tat* is that and refers to the Self, Brahman, *twam* means you and *asi* means are.

Tattva jnana: The knowledge of the fundamental truths or principles of existence. Refers to the realization or knowledge of the essence behind all appearances.

Trikala jnana: The knowledge of all three dimensions or aspects of time.

Upanishads: A collection of philosophical texts that form the core teachings of Hindu or Sanatan philosophy, especially the mystical and spiritual ideas behind the dharma. They explore the nature of reality, consciousness, self or atman, and the universal being, Brahman. Literally, Upanishad means sitting down near, implying learning in the presence of the Guru. The Upanishads deal with spiritual self-enquiry and search for the ultimate truth of life, self and existence.

Vedanta: A spiritual and philosophical tradition that focuses on understanding the nature of the Self, atman and its unity with the ultimate reality, Brahman. Literally, the end (anta) of knowing and knowledge (veda) in the Knower or the Self.

Vidya: Knowledge of truth; spiritual knowledge.

Vidyut: Explained in the story.

Vishnu: A name of Sri Krishna, a form of Narayan.

Yada yada hi dharmasya, glanir bhavati bharata, tadatmanam srjamyaham: From the Bhagavad Gita, Chapter 4, Verse 7, and means that whenever there is a decline in dharma, truth, righteousness, and a rise in adharma, that which opposes truth and righteousness, then I, Krishna, manifest Myself. This is the cosmic promise of the Divine: that whenever truth is endangered and chaos rises, the Divine takes form to restore balance.

Yoga: A methodized effort towards self-perfection by the expression of the potentialities latent in the being and union of the human individual with the universal and transcendent existence (Sri Aurobindo). Refers to inner union, integration or yoking together of the individual self with the universal Self, Brahman. Thus, any path, discipline or method that unites the seeker with the Self. A yogi (feminine, yogini) is one who practices yoga or lives in a yogic state, in union with the Self.

Yogaschittavritti nirodhah, tada drashtu swarupe avasthanam: Explained in the story.

About the Author

Partho practices Vedanta and is a disciple of Sri Aurobindo and the Mother. His inner journey started with a vision of Swami Vivekananda when he was twenty-six, and it was Swami Vivekananda who brought him to Sri Aurobindo and the Mother. He writes on Vedanta, mysticism, education and evolution.